A MAN YOU COULD
CALL A MAN

To Davidson College

[signature]

A MAN YOU COULD CALL A MAN

A Novel by

David G. Russell

CHAPEL HILL

FULL-SERVICE   BOOK-MAKERS
ESTD.   1999

PRESS

AUTHOR'S NOTE This is a work of fiction. All of the people are imagined, and anyone who suspects otherwise and tries to equate a character with a real person or part of a real person engages in idle speculation. Any similarity of a character's name with a real person's is purely coincidental. Likewise, all entities are imagined and cannot be equated with a real company, organization, or institution.

To David and Kelley,

*for the lives you will live
and the stories you will tell.*

CONTENTS

1

October 1972

TUESDAY The shadow of a cloud scurries up the hillside. Then it's gone, over the top and sliding down the backside. Soon others will chase it, up and gone as well, leaving the hemlock and mountain laurel in their wake.

Billy Burns gazes at the hillside but does not take account of the shadows. He sits and leans against the rough brick wall on the shipping dock of Quality Furniture, letting it scratch his back in the intermittent noonday sun. It's Tuesday but feels like it should be Friday. He closes his eyes only to see that damn eviction notice he got last week on the trailer door. I'll pay when I can, he had told them. He wanted to say when the fat lady sings, but wasn't sure it fit.

To shake the image, he picks up and flips through a day-old Asheville *Citizen-Times*. Flicking off a buzzing bee, he bites into a sandwich and washes it down with a gulp from his Thermos, a home-brew of equal parts Cheerwine and Jim Beam. A gust of wind carries his plastic sandwich bag away before he can smack it down on the concrete floor. He watches it tumble across the dusty asphalt, around the rear retreads of a company tractor-trailer. The truck's side is painted in color with a big picture of Don Harwood pointing his finger out at the world under a cartoony caption: *Don Delivers!*

Billy wipes his mouth with the back of his hand and looks back to see if anyone except Skin is within earshot. "Screw you, Don," he whispers into the wind.

Even as he approaches his one-year mark at the company, Billy has spoken to Don maybe twice, and only in passing. Mostly Don stays in the air-conditioned offices. That's fine by Billy, who keeps a low profile to keep his job, not wanting to trigger any further background checks. It's a wonder they were sloppy enough to miss so much the first time. He punches in and out on time, does his job more or less half-ass, and picks up his bi-weekly.

Just a few feet from Billy, Skin Johnson is stretched out from heel to bony shoulder blade on the cool concrete floor. One hand is tucked under his head as a pillow. The other helps anchor the sports section, folded like a little tent to shade his face.

Skin told Billy he got his name when he dropped out of the eleventh grade, losing weight when he didn't get free lunches anymore. He eats better now, but still has his skinny physique: six-one but 145 pounds, quite a contrast from the thick-necked, beer-bellied Billy. The two took to each other when Skin joined QF just six months ago. Skin even took to dressing like Billy, blue-jeaned and tee-shirted with shoulder-length hair, making them look like different sized twins. They stick together most days and nights, since Skin moved in with Billy for the time being, until he can spring for his own place and his own wheels.

Billy focuses on the paper. The national section trumpets how Nixon is supposed to clobber McGovern in a month, which Billy hopes will mean everyone can finally can get put out of their misery and never have to read about those two numbskulls again. He tosses the national aside and lazily picks up the local. There, on the front page, looking right at him again, is his boss Don, this time in black-and-white and not looking so goofy as on the truck.

In the photo, Don and his wife Carrie are all dressed up, like they just came from church. They wear forced grins and you can almost hear the photographer say "cheese!" There's a kid between them, holding a fishbowl, who the caption identifies as their son Matthew. The sun flashes and Billy feels the heat. He squints to read:

> Businessman Don Harwood, who owns Quality Furniture, and his wife Carrie have just announced a major contribution to the River Friends Society to save the endangered snail darter from becoming another victim of the polluted French Broad River.

Billy chuckles to himself. Don must not have told the reporter how much glue he pumps into that river every day.

He reaches back to pick at the mole on the nape of his neck; he's had it since before he checked into Craggy Correctional, and it seems to be getting bigger, darker, and more irritating. He tries not to think about it. He tells himself it's nothing, but can't help worrying that it has wormed itself deep into him. How could he know? He can't see it. Maybe it's going down his spine. Maybe it's growing into his brain. He shakes his head like a wet dog and assures himself that as long as his spit is still clear, he's ok.

> At this Saturday's fundraiser at the Grove Park Inn, Mr. and Mrs. Harwood will present a check in the amount of $100,000 to the Society and try to enlist other concerned environmentalists to pitch in for this once-in-a-lifetime rescue mission.

Billy sets the paper down and rubs his eyes with his knuckles. He shakes his head again. Then he picks up the paper and mouths the words: "Mr. and Mrs. Harwood will present a check in the amount of $100,000."

Billy kicks the sole of the Red Wing boot at the end of Skin's outstretched leg.

Skin stirs with a groan. "I was out, man. Why'd you...."

"Skin, you won't believe this shit. Our good buddy Don is giving away $100,000 to save a piss-ant fish!"

"What?" Skin slowly rouses. He pulls the sports section to the side and props himself up with his elbows.

Billy jabs his index finger at the article. "Don is giving away $100,000—that's *one hundred thousand dollars*—for a little see-through fish!"

Skin had been dreaming of running down the gravel shoulder of a road, trying to turn his head back enough to get a good look at who was chasing him. Billy slaps the paper down with a whack, snapping Skin out of his vision.

Billy scratches his back against the rough brick wall again. "How much does Don pay his workers?"

"You don't need me to tell you that. One sixty per hour, every hour, eight hours a day, 40 hours a week. And then they take out taxes and some other stuff and you take out the rent, and then I'm left with nothing but little deer droppings. Is this another one of your quizzes?" Skin's right eye twitches. He's had the tic ever since his forearm got bit by a rattler at a Pentecostal church outside of Newport in East Tennessee on what became his last day of attending any kind of religious service.

"Let's say you were a measly little fish. What would you do with 100 grand? You could even split it with another fish, so say it's 50."

"Geez. That's so far beyond stupid I don't know what to say."

"Come on."

Skin squats up and holds his stubbled chin in his hand. He looks sideways to the sunlight alternating on the hillside above the trucks. He figures he'll humor Billy. Skin doesn't want to be a total suck-up or anything, but the guy is his ride and room, for now. "Ok. I'd get a fast car and a fast woman and head to Florida. I might take Whataburger Betty. We'd smoke weed morning, noon, and night and every day for breakfast we'd drink fresh orange juice with vodka."

"Shit. If you take Betty, she'll take a third of Buncombe County with her, some way or another."

"You got me there. So I guess I'll take the new girl at Willie's." Willie's is their home-away-from-home on the west side, with cold Pabst Blue Ribbon and decent pool tables.

The lunchtime-is-over bell rings, and the two get up to return to the bowels of the furniture plant. Billy rips out the article about Don, folds it neatly, and puts it in his pocket.

With the Don article festering in his pocket, Billy works his afternoon shift like a robot. He never needs to think too much to do his job of lifting and moving. But today, more than most, his begrudging mind churns. Orphaned when he was three and raised, if you can call it that, by his uncle, he grew up resenting kids who had real parents. His uncle did what was required of him, but nothing more, to feed and clothe and eventually send him to school. He fell a little short on imparting the difference between right and wrong, which had a history of landing Billy in trouble. First it was picking fights at school, then suspensions, then truancy, then burglary, which sent him to Craggy Correctional for what was supposed to be a year of rehabilitation but ended out mostly stoking his smoldering resentment and giving him inmate-to-inmate education on how not to get caught next time.

Billy's mind still smolders, as three o'clock turns into four. He remembers Jesse, a guy he met the week before they let him out. He remembers walking the perimeter of the yard inside the chain-link fence, completing his routine of six rounds. He sat down on the ground to mind his own business before the horn blew. Only a week left of good behavior and he would be out of there and free. Just keep to yourself and no trouble, he repeated to himself. Somebody looked at him the wrong way, he'd look away, walk away. No trouble. One week. Seven days. Then his uncle would pick him up and they'd drive to the nearest 7-Eleven and get the coldest beer they have and maybe some beef jerky.

New guy, black as coal, sat beside him, failing to appreciate that Billy just wanted to be left alone.

Black guy had a white cloth tag with capital letters spelling out JESSE stitched onto his pocket, so there's no need for introductions. "What you in for?"

Billy wanted to say fuck off leave me alone but it's just seven days left so he said, "Burglary. You?"

"Attempted murder. Som bitch lived."

The two stared straight ahead, while the roofline shadow slid slowly across the bleak ground.

Three guards came out, hands on hips, ready to grab a Billy stick, as they usually did a minute or so before the horn.

Jesse and Billy stared at them.

Jesse, not pointing at them but lifting his head up just slightly in their direction to make clear to Billy he's talking about them, said under his voice: "They up. You down. What's up, gonna fall. What's down, gonna rise. Sure as the sun rise. The revolution is now, brother. It has to be now, 'cause if it's 50 or 100 years from now, what good's it gonna do you."

Then he stood up and slapped the dust from his trouser legs before starting for the line-up to trudge back inside.

Jesse looked down. "You wit me?" he asked Billy.

Billy got up and followed him in the line, confused why the guy had singled him out, and why he said what he did. That was the one and only time he saw Jesse. He must have been moved to a different section.

But somehow, even now, he can't get Jesse's words out of his head: "What's up, gonna fall. What's down, gonna rise." They cycle through Billy's head all the way to the end of the afternoon shift at QF.

He and Skin wait in line for the punch clock to tick from 4:59 to 5:00, then they are out the door swiftly and into Billy's 1964, jacked-up, two-door Impala coupe.

Skin reaches for the radio knob before he rolls a joint. This is standard protocol, but today, Billy isn't having it.

"Not now," Billy instructs. Older by three years than Skin, and his landlord in their single-wide, Billy is used to giving instructions to Skin. And Skin is used to following, for now.

"What's up?" Skin inquires.

"Something's been eating at me all afternoon. That article about Don and the 100 grand. The more I think about it, the more pissed I get."

"It's his money, man. You can't tell him what to do with it."

"Well, that's what's eating at me. Maybe I can. Maybe we can. What's up, gonna fall, and what's down, gonna rise."

"You ain't even toked and you're talking stupid again."

"Remember I asked you what you'd do with half of 100 grand? Fast car, fast woman, Florida, screwdrivers for breakfast?"

"Yeah. So what?"

"You forgot sunshine, feet in warm sand, and, and here's the best part, *never* having to work for Don or anyone else again!"

"I guess you must've finished your Thermos and brought an extra one today."

"This is serious, dork-head. Now, listen carefully. If you were Don, and you had so much money that you'd easily pay $100,000 to save a little fish, wouldn't you have no problem with paying the same amount to save your son?"

"I'm not following, dude. Who said his son needs saving? Is he sick?"

"No. He's a handsome, healthy boy. Ten or so. Curly blond hair. Dimples. That's the point. Gotta be worth as much as a fancy minnow."

"Look, you're talking shit, man. Let's do the number and turn on some tunes."

"Hold on a second. After a little planning and scouting, this will be easy. When Mr. and Mrs. Harwood are at that ball on Saturday night, we borrow the boy and leave a little note saying you can have him back for the price of a fish. We won't hurt him, just hold onto him for a couple of days while Don goes to the bank. Then we trade the boy for a boxful of tax-free twenties. Then we lie low for a couple of months, so they don't think it's us, then we're out of here, never to return. We're up, livin' the life of Riley in the Sunshine State."

"You've got to be fucking out of your mind! *Kidnapping?!* Man, how long has it been since you rolled off parole? I thought you said you'd never go back to Craggy!" Skin's eye twitches again.

"First of all, that was for burglary, which this isn't, and I was just an accomplice. Second, this isn't really kidnapping. We're just borrowing the boy for a couple of days and we're not going to get caught. That's the degree I earned at Craggy, not getting caught. No harm, no foul, and then we're rich. Think on it. I could do this all by myself, or I could split it even-steven with you. Think about it. The girl from Willies, endless weed, no more punch clocks, . . . Just think on it a little. Now, pass that joint. Are we out of beer?"

Skin is too stupefied to answer. He flicks on the lighter and they spark the joint. A few minutes pass before Skin turns on Asheville's "Classic Rock." After a commercial barking about discounts on Toyotas, the DJ says they are continuing the 1965 countdown with Eric Burdon and the Animals... Bum bum ba-bum bum, bum bum ba-bum bum ...Skin starts to jut his chin out with the beat.

As the song rises, Skin and Billy lower the windows and scream out the their favorite line: we gotta get out of this place!

Billy rides on, feeling invincible. Almost floating. Feeling the plan is so simple it's air-tight.

Skin is thinking on it, wondering if this is just Billy spoofing him.

They ride on, semi-stoned and speechless, until, as always, they break out laughing when they pass by the Federal Credit Union. On the second-story roof of the building is a billboard that reads: "Jesus Saves."

They're full of giggles until Billy cuts the motor off in front of the trailer and sees a piece of paper duct-taped to the front door. In the fading light, he has to walk right up to it to read the big letters: SECOND EVICTION NOTICE, under which a lot of little letters blur together.

He spits on the paper, rips it out of the tape, wads it up, and throws it at Skin.

"God dammit to hell! We gotta get out of this place!"

———

WEDNESDAY Don leans back in his black leather upholstered chair such that his head is directly under the wood-mounted speckled trout. It used to be fourteen pulsing inches of muscle before it flicked its tail fin up from a dark pool at the sparkling speed of light, opened its pink jaws, and bit into one fly too many, ending its idyllic life in the cool waters that cascade green and white over the rounded boulders that punctuate Snake Creek.

Don is a regular looking guy, medium build, with brown hair parted neatly on the right side, dressed in a shirt and tie, with the coat hanging behind the door. Within the last year, he has started to let his sideburns grow an extra quarter inch down his face, something that his late father, photographed and framed on the side wall, frowns on. But then again his father is always frowning at something, even ten years ago when he co-signed the loan that let Don borrow the money to buy a furniture business. Don doesn't know why he keeps the photo hanging there looking down on him. It always makes him feel small, like a boy in shorts.

The sideburns are Don's only hint at rebellion. Otherwise, he is a well-respected, rule-following, confrontation-avoiding family man in Asheville, running a business, paying his people, keeping current on his debts, attending church most Sundays, joining do-good civic organizations, abiding by the law, and occasionally grilling hamburgers out in the backyard on weekends. At the worship services at First Baptist, he stands for hymns but never sings. Even so, he wells up at *I come to the garden alone, while the dew is still on the roses, and the voice I hear falling on my ear, the Son of God discloses, ... and He walks with me, and He talks with me, and he tells me I am His own.* Once or twice he almost moved to walk down the aisle, until he restrained any sort of public show of emotion, inconspicuously lifting a finger to dab a tear under the guise of rubbing his eye.

Like everyone else in Buncombe County over the age of 21, with the exception of a few college professors and his wife Carrie, he is a registered Republican who sees no problem with the national ticket. When Carrie confronts him about whether he's really going to vote for Nixon, he disengages or walks away, avoiding a clash with her, especially if Matthew is around.

Like on the side of the QF truck, Don is a two-dimensional man. He can go up-down and right-left all day long. But don't probe his depth. And for God's sake don't try to get a religious or political or personal opinion from him; he'll change the subject and sit back down in his seat on the sidelines watching the game. It suits him to stay neutral and nice.

Don is a man of the cleared land, land that has been divided up and parceled out and fenced around. He is more comfortable so situated than in the wild, although, witness the trout, he sometimes tries his hand at controlled adventure. He is the kind of man who stops at yellow lights. He is always early and never underdressed. He is this way because that is how his father laid down the law when Don was growing up. "Always stay between the ditches, son," his father would harp, "because if you swerve too far to either side you may not be able to get out."

Don glances at the photo on the wall. His father is as remote hanging there as he was in life. Not that they didn't spend time together, but they never seemed to connect. It was like Don was an electron circling the nucleus of his father, pushed and pulled into equilibrium such that a coming together, much less a collision, was not possible under the laws of nature as applied to them.

Don vows to do differently by his own son.

The translucent glass on the upper half of the door darkens and Don hears a *knock-knock*.

"Come in."

In walks Wally Deleau, the operations manager, whom Don summoned for a serious conversation that likely will bear on Wally's year-end, discretionary bonus. The two sit across Don's wide, custom-made, wormy chestnut desk.

Wally sees the row of paperclips on the desk that have all been unfolded and reworked into the shape of fish hooks. Don fiddles with another one and counts: one, two, three, four, five, six, seven—this one makes eight. Before he realizes he's doing it, Don counts things, like steps he climbs, or seconds when he's holding his breath, but today it's fish hooks.

Wally asks, "Busy day?"

"Every day is a busy day. I'm busy thinking right at this moment, and I'll tell you what about." Don pauses to flick some lint off of his trouser leg. "You know that I have always been able to count on you. You've been here, what, five years now?"

"Seven."

"Well, I have a special assignment for you." Don hooks his right thumb up to point back to the now-indifferent trout. "You remember how you taught me to fly fish?"

"Sure. You were a natural. Didn't need much teaching." Wally hopes Don didn't catch the sarcasm that edged into his voice unbidden. If anything, Don is not a natural.

"My boy's ten, and I think it's time he learned. It'd be something he can enjoy his entire life, if he takes to it."

"Has he taken to other sports? Baseball? Basketball?"

Don hesitates. He hasn't expected this question, and a blue hue seeps into his conscience for not taking the time that some other dads do to coach a team or help his son learn a sport.

"Not so much. I don't know why. He does a lot of stuff by himself. His mother paints, and he draws. I'm not saying he's a Mama's boy, but I just want to give him something that he and I can do together. You know, a manly kinda thing. Fishing would be good, right?"

"I don't see many women out there doing it in the streams." Wally is the only one to crack a smile.

"I thought about a rod for Christmas, and then you could give him some lessons after that on how to tie a fly and cast. You could do that in our backyard, and then maybe the three of us could do a weekend out on the river."

"You want me to help you pick out the gear? Be cheaper if we mail order."

"That's what I was going to ask you. Thanks."

"So, if you don't mind me asking, does he have more patience than you?"

"Ha! You're a funny guy. Now tell me what's up with the new design."

"I'd rather show you."

Wally and Don walk out of the office, down the hall, and into the shop, where Wally and his team are experimenting with substituting hardwood with plywood and particle board in places that the customer won't easily see, in the name of cost-effective production.

"This is all cool, isn't it?" Don asks Wally.

"Sure...."

"Because we don't need another...."

"Yeah, I got it. We don't need another fucking problem."

Don frowns at Wally's loose tongue but does not rebuke him.

Wally apologizes anyway, his enthusiasm tempered.

Don turns to him and says, "Well, what I was going to say is that we need to be careful. All the time. With what we say and what we do. No reason to mess up the good thing we have going."

"Just a suggestion, boss."

Dons walks back to his office alone. He sees the row of paperclip hooks and wonders what Matthew is doing at school.

———

Fourth-grade afternoon recess is teacher-supervised in name only. The teacher sits in the shade next to the building with her head buried in a magazine, while the kids play kick ball on the thin, patchy grass field.

Matthew Harwood is playing second base with a runner on first and one out. The kicker at the plate is the biggest, roughest boy in the class, new this fall to the school, after being held back a year at his old school across the county. His toe catches the ball too low, and he launches a high, shallow, fly ball. Matthew loses it in the blinding October sun, and the ball passes between his outstretched arms and socks him in the face, knocking his glasses off, before it rolls several feet behind him. He scrambles to it, grabs it amid the dust clouds, and turns toward the runner, who had hesitated, thinking the ball would be caught.

Not seeing well without his glasses, Matthew stumbles as he lunges to make the tag, overshooting and unintentionally knocking the runner hard to the ground. Matthew stands over him and meekly says, "Sorry."

That apology is unheard by the kicker, who is upset with himself for his puny at-bat. He runs over full-speed from first base, extends his arms straight out, and rams into Matthew's shoulders, sending him backwards to a painful landing on his tailbone.

"Get up!" he yells.

Matthew rolls over and rubs his lower back. Then he gets on his hands and knees, only to feel the solid thud of a kick to his left thigh.

"Get up, Miss Priss!" By this time, the big, rough boy has balled his fists and starts to circle Matthew, who just sits there in disbelief. He has never been in a fight before. A couple of his friends, led by Paul, start to form a barrier of protection.

"I said I was sorry," Matthew shrieks, his voice coming out higher pitched than normal.

"Prissy, pretty boy! You scared?"

Still stunned at the quick turn of events, Matthew stands up, looks the other boy in the eye, and lies, "No, I'm not scared of you." He turns his back and walks off the field, hoping at every step that the bully will not charge him.

He doesn't. He screws up his face and asks the others, "what're you looking at?" Then he kicks the dust and feels about as stupid as he is.

The teacher sees Matthew heading in with head down and does not notice his red face. She asks him what's up, to which Matthew, holding back a quivering tongue, replies, as evenly as he can, "Nothing. Just gotta go to the bathroom."

After gathering himself in the boys' room, Matthew looks at the clock on the hallway wall and sees that it is not that long—maybe even a time period he can tolerate—before school is out.

———————

Carrie Harwood has just under an hour before she picks Matthew up. In her home studio she tries to finish a watercolor of a blue-gray blue jay bending over to sip from a beige birdbath. She moves quickly before the paint dries, knowing from experience that less is more if she is to capture the light and movement, and that overworking the piece will burden and ruin it. She wears a splotched cotton apron, which she pulls up to dab some of the darkness away from the bird's back.

When she was in high school at Ashley Hall in Charleston, her art teacher encouraged her to find ways to express herself beyond the frozen realism of Elizabeth O'Neill Verner's sketches and paintings, which Carrie had started to copy. Now, after painting a few hours most every day since Matthew started kindergarten, she has learned not draw all the lines or connect all the dots. She puts down just enough to suggest the essence of, say, a brown thrasher peering from behind a magnolia blossom, or a red-bellied woodpecker gripping a swaying dogwood branch.

The focal point of each of her paintings is the bird's eye. She has mastered it as the all-knowing, all-seeing, see-right-through-you, sun-bright, searing eye like the one on the top of the pyramid on the back of a dollar bill. When you look at it, it looks right back, knowing whether you are worthy or unworthy.

How she came to this she won't say. Certainly not to Don. Early on she would show him her work and he just wouldn't get her subtlety. "Nice bird," he might say.

She won't say, but she knows. She has memorized the thirteen stanzas of Wallace Stevens's poem but repeats aloud only the first one: "Among twenty snowy mountains, / The only moving thing / Was the eye of the blackbird." The eye of that poem follows her everywhere, as she moves among the mountains that surround Asheville.

Sometimes, when she is totally immersed in the eye, she paints it like it's a raindrop that clings to a leaf, the kind that when you go right up close in the softest light of early morning, you see the world upside down.

When Carrie paints, she feels like she is giving life, investing a part of herself into each of her works. She refuses offers to buy her watercolors or to exhibit them. They are her true friends, and she cannot bear the thought of letting them go. Some she frames and hangs in the kitchen or the hallway. Others she keeps in her portfolio binder. They keep her company when otherwise she would be alone.

"You're done," she says to the blue jay, who stares back at her. "You might even make it to the wall in the den."

"Oh, Carrie, that would be so wonderful!" Carrie hears the bird respond with a mocking voice.

"Hey, buddy, you wouldn't even be here but for me. So try to act nice like good bird, ok?"

"Sure. Sorry. Isn't it time for you to pick up Matthew?"

Carrie looks at her watch. "Oh, you're right. Better go. And remember, this conversation is just between you and me. We don't want to connect all the dots."

Carrie stirs her brushes in the coffee cup of gray water and pats and squeezes them with her apron, which she unties and tosses to the counter. Then she combs her hand through her short, semi-blond hair, reapplies her lipstick, straightens her skirt, grabs the keys out of her purse, locks the door, and drives her yellow VW Beetle to the elementary school. By now, she is used to the incredulous looks she gets from people who spot her blue-and-white McGovern Shriver '72 bumper sticker.

———————

THURSDAY Matthew's right upper teeth pounded in his head all day at school. He could hardly hear the discussion on the architecture of the Mayans. After the pain would not go away, he told his teacher, who called Carrie, who pressured the dentist's receptionist to get him in today.

Now Matthew reclines in the wide chair and tries to relax his stiff body as the dentist scrapes sharp metal tools across his teeth. The searing pain shoots immediately through his skull when the tool hits the bad tooth.

"Looks like you've got your first cavity, son. It's your second molar, top right. Surprised you haven't had one earlier." The dentist backs away on his rolling stool, sounding calm and friendly. "Here's what we're going to do. First, we'll take an x-ray of your entire set of teeth. You haven't had one done in two years. Then we'll give you a little shot so you won't feel anything when we clean it out and put the silver filling in. You'll be out of here in an hour, as good as new."

Matthew says ok, as he really isn't being asked to make a decision.

He tries to unclench his fists and breathe as the assistant drapes the heavy apron over him and points the big yellow plastic cone at his cheek. Before the shot and the filling, they show him the black-and-white x-rays and tell him that every set of teeth is unique, like fingerprints. After the procedure is over, they take one more x-ray, focused on the new filling.

On the way home, Carrie buys him a small chocolate shake. Even with the straw, it drools down his chin, as his lips won't close quite right. "The Zulicks' golden retriever had puppies last night. Do you want to swing by to see them?" She asks, to which Matthew nods yes.

Matthew has never seen a litter before. He is fascinated by how small and white and fuzzy the puppies are, compared to their dark-honey, long-haired mother. Through numb lips, he says, "They have boo eyes!" The word *blue* won't quite come out right.

"Yes, like you. But their eyes will turn brown, and yours will be blue forever."

"Can we have one, please?"

"Well, that's a bigger job than you think, but we'll ask Daddy. Anyway, these pups have to stay with their mother for about six weeks."

"So, we could bring one home just before Thanksgiving?"

———

At 5:00, Billy and Skin check out of work, drop by Willie's to kill some time and a couple of beers, and then proceed into the softening evening to scout out where the Harwoods live. Billy has torn out of the pay phone book the white page that shows their address and home phone number.

He turns off of Charlotte Street and onto the counterclockwise loop of Sunset Parkway. They both look for 46. Skin is closer to the mailboxes, so he reads out the numbers: 70, 64, 58. Billy slows down and parks in front of 52, which looks like it's undergoing a major renovation. Both of them sit in silence as they survey the scene.

The amber sunlight leans in through the trees.

Billy is the first to speak. "Beautiful."

Skin agrees, "This is probably the prettiest neighborhood I've ever seen, and to think people actually live here. Don lives here."

"No. I ain't talking about that. Look at the house right here, right next to Don's."

"Yeah. So what?"

"It's being fixed up in a big way. Nobody could live there with all that stuff going on. And there's the bonanza—look at all those ladders stacked up between the houses. This is a good omen, Skin, things are working out just like we want them to."

Just then, they see a light come on in an upstairs room on the side of Don's house that faces the house under construction. A window in the room opens, and a boy with glasses looks out.

Billy smiles.

———

FRIDAY As the cook clears off the table, Carrie hands the Waldorf salad dish up to her. Then she sees Mrs. Ayers, the impertinent one, hold up the book *My Name is Asher Lev* by Chaim Potok, and ask "which one of you so-called ladies chose this God-awful book? I couldn't get past the first three chapters. Those people are so... repulsive!"

The hostess for this month's lunch, Mrs. Wolfe, is quick to reply, "You know I chose it. The hostess always chooses. And it got a very good write-up in the *New York Times*."

"The what?" Mrs. Ayers is not impressed. "So now you're not only turning Jewish but McGovernish as well?"

"I like reading about foreign people who have moved to America," Mrs. Wolfe says. "Not that I want to be one of them, of course. But it makes me appreciate that they're human, too."

"Jesus, save me from these liberals!" Exclaims Mrs. Ayers.

"The salad was lovely, Janine. What's next?" asks Mrs. Whetsell, trying to bring everybody back to common ground.

"Reuben sandwiches and a kosher pickle!" Mrs. Wolfe proudly announces. "It took me a while to think of something that was Brooklyn Jewish that you ladies would like."

"Do you have any Brooklyn Schnapps?" deadpans Mrs. Ayers.

Carrie breaks her silence. "I think y'all are missing the point. What got to me was the story of a boy who was born sensitive but who turned out to be brave enough to pursue his own passion, which was art, even if it meant offending his parents or his rabbi." She thinks of her son sketching every day, drawing pencil portraits of her and Don, imaginary landscapes, still-lifes of a bowl of oranges or a pyramid of apples. There is an edginess about his talent that she doesn't quite understand.

The other ladies look at Carrie as if she just defected to Brooklyn. Carrie puts on like she does not really care.

"Think about it. It's a story of a family suffering. But obviously no one at this table knows much about this because we lead perfect lives and everything goes according to plan."

The living room becomes so silent that all anyone can hear is the cook in the kitchen humming as she puts the corned beef and sauerkraut on toasted rye slathered with mustard.

Carrie feels the pressure in her head swelling. She massages her temples. She hears Matthew call out for her. Mommy?

"Not now, sweetie," she says. Then, to the ladies, "Excuse me. I forgot something… and I've got to go."

After Carrie closes the door behind her, Mrs. Ayers looks around the table and shakes her head. "Did you notice, or is it just me, but something's just not right about that woman."

At QF, the afternoon hours proceed in slow motion. Billy and Skin agree to make the day appear like business as usual, but Skin is jittery and unusually eye-twitchy. His hands are so sweaty that he loses his grip on a chest of drawers, which hits the hard floor with a loud crack. Skin cannot see any damage, so the piece goes into the truck.

After work, they have errands. Billy stays in the car while Skin, as instructed, walks into Belk's and looks for the women's department. This is uncharted territory for him, and he feels a tingly sense of perversion when he finds himself in the lingerie aisle, surrounded by every item imaginable except what he has been tasked to buy: regular black stockings. They are nowhere to be found. All Belk's seems to carry is pantyhose.

Skin finally breaks down and asks a sales clerk, "My wife sent me to find stockings. Can you help?"

"We may have a few in back. What size?"

Skin is stumped. He doesn't know they come in sizes. "36," he responds.

"They only come in small, medium, and full-figure."

"Sorry. Medium."

It takes ten minutes before he gets the package, pays cash for it, and heads out.

"What the hell took you so long?" Billy barks.

"Had to try them on." Billy is not in a humorous mood. They now have just 30 minutes before the hardware store closes.

Billy decides he'll handle this assignment, and he efficiently finds and buys duct tape, rope, rubber gloves, a flashlight, and a short garden hose.

All that's left is the liquor store and the gas station, and then they'll be set—set to smoke a few, drink a few, and just generally chill so that they don't get too fritzed-out about what tomorrow may bring.

Friday evening at the Harwoods' means dinner at 7:00. Carrie cooks while Don watches the CBS Evening News with Walter Cronkite in the den. She knows it's over when she hears, "and that's the way it is, Friday, October 6…" followed by the click of Don switching the TV off.

He lazily walks into the kitchen scratching his head. "I think I dozed off a bit."

"Well, what's the news?"

"I only caught part of it, but there was a big train wreck in Mexico that killed over 200 pilgrims."

"I thought the pilgrims lived in Massachusetts?"

"It's really not something to joke about. The scene was awful. Those poor families. Can you imagine getting a call out of the blue saying 'I'm sorry to inform you that…'"

"No. I can't. Can you call Matthew in? I'm almost done."

Don walks out the front door into the dimming, peaceful twilight and down the blue-stone steps to the sidewalk, flanked by two cedar trees that stand as tall and solid as sentries guarding his stately home. He sees Matthew in the park inside the loop of Sunset Parkway. He and the other neighborhood children are having a pine-cone grenade skirmish. They run and hide behind tree trunks or bushes and then attack by hurling the cones, which, due to their light weight, only travel about 20 feet. So far, it appears no one is in danger, unless the grenades start to actually explode.

"Matthew… dinner."

"Ok. Just a second."

Friday is the only day of the week when Carrie fixes a big meal. She can't remember how or why that family tradition started. After she returned from the book club, she painted for an hour (asking a cardinal why he was pecking at a worm and receiving the question why not in return), started the pot roast by searing the beef and then putting the gas flame on low, picked Matthew up, and stopped by Ingles for what she needed.

Don reenters the kitchen. "He's coming."

Within a few minutes, Matthew comes in. His khaki pants have grass and dirt stains on both knees. He is panting like a puppy.

"Wash your hands." Carrie always says this.

The three of them sit down in their assigned seats at the dining room table, another Friday tradition. Other days they sit at the kitchen table.

"Matthew, it's your turn."

They bow their heads as Matthew offers a prayer: "Dear God, bless this food to the nourishment of our bodies and help those people who need help. In Jesus' name, I'm starving. Amen. I mean, in Jesus' name, Amen."

"This is a good night to be hungry," Carrie says, "we have pot roast, your favorite, gravy, boiled and buttered new potatoes, and squash casserole with saltines and cheddar cheese. And I got some buttermilk."

They pass the serving plates in silence at the dinner table, from mother to father to son, each a member of the family but each a unique person with his or her own mind and heart, each with a separate soul stirring inside, each with a different and unknowable future waiting to unfold. They are as tightly connected as any family could expect, yet apart, like the legs of the table at which they sit.

"Didn't you have your book club thing today?" Don asks.

"I did. You know that group. I tried to carry the conversation, like usual. But I had to leave early." Carrie starts to feel the pressure in her head again. "Not sure I want to continue doing it. How was work?"

"Ok. About the same as your book club, honestly. We had the marketing people come in and they want us to get a new slogan. They think 'Don Delivers' is not catchy enough, even though I kinda like it. They think we should sponsor a local TV show or the local news."

Matthew perks up. "You're going to be on TV?"

"Actually, I thought we'd have a handsome, ten-year old kid be our company spokesman. Know anybody who'd be interested?"

"Wow. That'd be cool."

"How was school today?"

"Fine."

"That's what you always say," Don said. "Anything happen to report on?"

"Nope. It was ok. Just the normal stuff."

Matthew's forehead knots up as he thinks of the week. He can see the blur of the boy circling him and his heart starts to pound. Maybe he should have pushed back. But what then? He was a lot bigger. He remembered being called a prissy, but he doesn't think he is one. He wonders if he should tell his Dad. Maybe not since it's all over anyway. What would his Dad do if some guy pushed him down?

They eat in silence until Carrie says, "Ok, Matthew. Time for your three questions." This also had grown into a Friday night tradition.

"Why do tomatoes turn red?"

Carrie looks at Don, who answers, "Same reason leaves do. Next."

"Can flies fly in the rain?"

"Of course not," Don is quick to respond. "Only a dry fly flies." He thinks of the fly rod that Wally is ordering and envisions father and son casting in a stream on a Saturday morning. "Last one."

"How long do butterflies live?"

Don looks to Carrie for this one.

"As long as they can."

Then Carrie starts to get up.

"If you two gentlemen will help with the dishes, I'll let you pick between the Brady Bunch and Sonny and Cher."

After the dinner, dishes, and the show, it's nine and time for Matthew to go to bed.

Don tells him goodnight from the kitchen, while Carrie goes up with him. He brushes his teeth, uses a wash cloth on his knees, and gets his pajamas on.

Carrie catches a whiff of boy odor when she's tucking him in and gently suggests: "You'll need to shower one of these days." She tucks him in and kisses his cheek. "You know that you'll always be Mommy's little prince of light, even though you're getting to be a big boy. Honestly, I don't know what I'd do without you."

Honestly, she doesn't, as her world can slip into darkness, like falling off a cliff, before she realizes what's happening.

"I don't plan on going anywhere."

Carrie leaves the door to the hall open so that the attic fan can pull the night air in through the bedroom window. She reminds herself to tell Don to fix the screen in his window, but forgets by the time she snuggles up next to him on the den sofa.

Matthew lies on his back and watches the light from the street lamps outside dance upside down on the ceiling, like yellow flames from candles when the air moves through them. The light is filtered by the swaying leaves, whose soft rush he can faintly hear. Occasionally, he also hears the droning of a car slowly passing by, and, fainter still, a car door shutting several houses away, followed by three rough barks from a distant dog.

He curls his body up and puts his left arm under the pillow. His right hand and forearm stick out above the covers, and the night breeze from the window drifts over the few hairs that are starting to emerge on his arm.

He wonders what it is like to be older. The boys in high school are giants, and they hang out with girls, like in the movies or on TV. His friend Paul told him what boys and girls supposedly do together in high school, but Matthew hardly believes it, like why would a boy want to wrestle a girl? The boys drive cars and play football, and, as Matthew has personally witnessed, they smoke in cars parked in his neighborhood and sometimes throw beer cans out onto the grass. After five more years—which might as well be a century—he'll be one of them. He feels intimidated by the prospect, but it's so hard to imagine that it all gets fuzzy, and he starts to slip into the deep, dreamy sleep that is the blessing and province of the young.

SATURDAY At two in the afternoon, while Carrie is still at the hairdress-
er, Don turns on the den TV and switches to NBC before he and Matthew
settle into the sofa for the first game of the National League Championship Series. The Cincinnati Reds have travelled to Three Rivers Stadium
in Pittsburgh to take on the Pirates. Don, a Reds' fan since he was a boy,
has almost converted Matthew by talking about the Reds' "redemption"
season—their stunning, redeeming success after a pitiful record in 1971.

Don and Matthew sip their Cokes, and they share the bag of Ruffles
potato chips that sits between them. Before they are halfway done with
the Cokes, the announcer Jim Simpson yells, "And that one's outta here!"
as Joe Morgan, in the top half of the first inning, crisply swings, connects
with the hardball, and trots the bases for a home run and a 1-0 early lead
by the Reds. Don tries to contain his joy but nonetheless embarrasses
himself by spewing chips onto the carpet. That is the only joyful moment,
as the Pirates regroup and ultimately take the game by a score of 5-1.

After it's over, Matthew consoles his father: "Hey, Dad, it's three out of
five, right? Tomorrow will be a 'redemption' day."

———————

In the living room, Matthew holds the Kodak camera up and frames his
parents in front of the brick fireplace. Don is tuxedoed, and Carrie wears a
gray, sequined gown. She is more eye-shadowed and lip-sticked than usual.

"One, two, three," Matthew calls out. *Flash!*

"Do one more," Carrie says, "my legs weren't in the right position."

"Your legs are not even in the frame, dear," Don responds.

"Do one anyway!"

Matthew starts to count again but is interrupted by a loud knocking at
the front door.

"Who on earth?" Don asks.

He opens the door to Becky the babysitter, holding a calculus text-
book, ten minutes early just like usual. Of the many blessings the Harwoods have, Becky is one of them. She lives three blocks away, goes to

their church, gets along great with Matthew, and is as trustworthy as they come.

"Good evening, Mr. and Mrs. Harwood. You both look super. Hey, Matt-Matt, how's it going?" Ever since she started sitting for Matthew four years ago, she has called him that, and he doesn't even mind.

"Well, since you're here, we can go. We'll be back no later than 10:30. Help yourself to the meatloaf."

"No, ma'am. I've had dinner already. But thanks anyway."

"Ok. Same drill. Lights out for him at nine, especially tonight. He's supposed to read a verse at the 11:00 o'clock service tomorrow. It's Youth Sunday."

"No problemo."

After Don and Carrie leave, Becky tells Matt-Matt, "Ok, here's the drill for tonight. I've got this big test on Monday so I'll need to study. So why don't you and I play a board game and then you can go upstairs?"

"Sure. Monopoly or Scrabble?"

———

At a shade before 9:00, after spending an hour at Willie's as part one of their alibi (should they ever need one), Billy and Skin glide in next to the curb on Sunset Parkway in front of the house being remodeled, about two car lengths from the Harwood's driveway. They both can see Matthew's window. His light is on and there is a single shadow of a movement. Then, at 9:05, the light goes out. They plan to wait fifteen minutes before making their approach.

"You cool, bro?" Billy whispers.

"Yep. Sure." Skin taps his fingers on his right thigh, at about ten beats a second. He's really not cool. He almost tells Billy he can have all this bullshit to himself. But then he has a vision of a boxful of twenties, half of which will be his, tax-free.

An early fall breeze runs through the neighborhood, and the oaks and poplars shiver. The hemlocks sway. Otherwise, all is still and quiet.

Each minute seems like it takes an hour.

Finally it is 9:15. Time to move.

Billy starts to open his door but sees a red car approaching from behind. It slowly passes him, turns out its lights, and parks just beyond the Harwoods' on the other side. A man, maybe just a teenager, gets out of a Mustang convertible and walks up to the Harwoods' front door, which opens before he's up the steps. He enters quickly and disappears behind the closed door.

Billy had figured there would be a babysitter, an unaccompanied babysitter.

"Shit! Who knew she had the balls to invite her boyfriend over!" Billy is surprisingly calm as he recalculates their plan.

Skin keeps tapping and doesn't respond. He's now hoping this is a joke and Billy won't actually do it.

"This could be good. She's distracted. This is better." Billy convinces himself.

Skin is waiting for Billy to throw in the towel so they can go back and get drunk at Willie's like usual.

But the words he hears are: "Let's go. No. Wait. Put on your stocking."

"Shit!" Skin whispers to himself. Then, with resignation, "What the fuck...."

They each slide a black stocking over their heads and arrange it so they can see through the holes they cut. Billy puts on his gloves.

"Now."

Billy and Skin walk furtively in their black tee-shirts to the hedge-row boundary next to the house being remodeled and gingerly lift the wooden ladder. They put two old socks on the top of the rails to dampen the sound, then tip-toe the ladder through the gape in the bushes. From there they can see straight into the den window, witnessing the unabashed groping and kissing on the sofa. As clearly as if they were in the same room, they hear the canned laughter on the Mary Tyler Moore

Show. They are transfixed for a moment, until Billy tugs at the ladder and they proceed to the ground under Matthew's window. They raise the ladder as if handling a bomb that might explode any second. It now rests evenly against the brick on the side of the house, almost touching the window sill. So far, so good.

Inside the open window, Matthew is dead asleep under a down comforter. As usual, his door to the hallway is open to allow the droning, lulling attic fan to pull in the sweet autumn night air, which sweeps around the room and floats through the boy's golden hair before taking its leave.

Billy begins his slow ascent, hand over hand, with feet to follow, while Skin anchors the ladder by holding its rails.

As Billy's head reaches the window sill, he can feel the current of cool air being sucked in. He starts to be seduced by the peace of the place and, for a brief moment, remembers a childhood night dozing off under quilts. But then he snaps back and bucks up into action.

Like a python, he slithers hands and head first into the semi-dark room, which is faintly illuminated by a night light plugged into the baseboard.

He stands on the floor, a few feet from the bed and the slumbering child, before taking slow, purposeful steps to shut the door to the hallway. On his last step, the floorboard creaks, and he freezes. No noticeable reaction in the room or downstairs, where the TV laughter can still be heard.

He returns to the bedside. This is the hardest part, and he knows it all has to go perfectly.

He pulls out the pistol and the cardboard sign and taps Matthew on the shoulder of his pajamas.

No response.

Billy squeezes the boy's small tricep lightly, and then harder.

Matthew turns and mutters, "What?" His ragged teddy bear is knocked to the floor.

Then his eyes flash open as he sees the man with the black stocking over his head and a gun and a sign: KEEP QUIET OR YOU DIE.

Instinctively Matthew starts to curl up into a protective ball, almost a fetal position.

"Turn over," Billy whispers.

Matthew can't understand because the stocking mutes the words. He smells the heavy smell of beer on Billy's breath.

Billy leans in, gun first, and repeats into Matthew's ear, "Turn over."

Matthew complies.

Billy sets the pistol on the bedside table on top of Matthew's sketchbook and wraps duct tape around the boy's head, first as a gag and then as a blindfold. Then he yanks the boy's hands behind him and tapes those together. He'll do the feet later, if need be.

"Get up."

Matthew is frozen into a ball.

Billy leans in again. "Get up, *now*."

The boy slides his legs off the bed and stands. Billy turns him to face the window. "You're going down the ladder first. I'll guide your feet to the rungs."

Matthew panics. He twists and breaks free and tries blindly to make for where the door should be. Behind the gag, he screams, which comes out as *"Uhhh...ummmm...uhhhh!!"*

Billy quickly reaches out and catches Matthew's taped hands. He jerks him around and grabs and pulls his hair with his left hand and slaps Matthew hard in the face with his right. The blow knocks Matthew down, and he folds over on the side of the bed.

Billy pulls Matthew's head by the hair and pushes his mouth next to the boy's ear. *"Shut...the...fuck...up!* Do you hear me?"

Matthew trembles but manages to nod.

Billy listens. No steps. No movement. He picks up his pistol and presses the cold barrel against Matthew's neck.

"No funny business or I shoot." Billy has the odd sensation that he's reading corny lines from some movie. He puts his note on the bedside table next to Matthew's glasses. He leads Matthew back to the window and stands him on the second rung from the top.

"Easy boy. One step at a time."

But Matthew is blind and terrified. He misses the next step and falls one story down with all of his weight on Skin, who sees him coming, lets go of the ladder, and tries to catch him. The result of which is the full force of 70 pounds smacking them both to the ground. The thud is drowned out by the TV's canned laughter.

"Fuck!" Billy whispers, tasting the nylon of his mask.

He descends as quickly and quietly as he can down the ladder and stands both Skin and Matthew up.

They hear Bob Newhart, more canned laughter, then the boyfriend groaning.

Billy tells himself that the hard part is over, for now. They collar Matthew, lead him to the Impala, and place him in its spacious trunk, which is now equipped with four inches of garden hose to allow the air in from the back seat.

Billy turns the key and mumbles, "I told you it'd be easy."

He takes off the stocking and eases out of the neighborhood.

Skin resumes his thigh-tapping. His hands tremble as he flicks the lighter to the tip of the joint he'd rolled for this moment.

Billy drives back to Willie's for part two of their alibi. They keep Matthew in the trunk with the hose air vent and go in for a beer and a Penrose pickled sausage each. Billy sees a girl who's not one of the regulars. She's wearing a white mini-skirt and a tank top, leaning against the wall and watching the guys play pool. Skin, feeling too anxious to move, stays at the bar while Billy moves over and leans next to her. After pretending to watch the game, he lowers his right arm and reaches to the very top of the back of her bare left leg and squeezes it. She backs away and turns to him with a "you son of a ...." Billy just grins at her.

A man who must have been her friend, another non-regular and six inches taller than Billy, comes over holding his cue stick diagonally across his body, ready to flick the fat end up into Billy's face. Billy raises both hands in surrender and apologizes for the interruption. By now, Willie is on the scene and breaks things up.

"Shit, I didn't mean anything," Billy says to Willie, who replies, "Sure, of course not, just putting your hand up her dress not meaning anything by it. You got a screw loose? Why don't you and Skin call it a night."

It's a little after 11:00 before Billy and Skin pay up and head out.

In the parking lot, Skin confronts Billy, "You *jackass!* Why're you trying to cause trouble and draw attention to us when we just pulled the shit we pulled? What the hell are you thinking?"

"Come on Skin, don't be an idiot. That's exactly what I was trying to do. This way Willie has something to remember about us being here this night. Just in case."

"Well, how 'bout cluing me in next time, mister? I thought we were supposed to be doing this together. I need to know what's going on, ok? Or maybe I bail."

"Too late for that, buddy-roo." Billy accelerates as he hits the road and burns just enough rubber to make a punctuation mark.

———

Three miles north, at the storied Grove Park Inn, a granite resort once graced by the likes of Scott and Zelda Fitzgerald, the Harwoods acknowledge the accolades, smile for pictures, shake hands with ex-Mayor Montgomery, and dance cheek-to-cheek to a jazz combo. The crowd includes wealthy businessmen, insurance brokers, bankers, lawyers, and doctors, the kind of people who can afford to give away hunks of money to get a notch up in their prestige in the community. When she's on her game, Carrie can fit in more easily than Don and can play the part of being the belle of the ball, owing to her debutante days in Charleston to her reign as homecoming queen at the all-male Wofford College when she was a junior at the all-female Converse. Don, with his blue-collar and green-collard roots in Statesville, is always trying to adapt, but he can't help feeling like a mixed breed in a pedigree show.

Don and Carrie have one-too-many whiskey sours. With each drink, they think that they look and dance better. Carrie could hardly look better; her figure hasn't changed since college, and her face remains soft and young. Don, the regular-looking guy, is starting to show some age and pudge, but he figures that is good for business, and what's good for business is good for Don. They stay later than they had planned, and it is 10:30 before they try to find their Lincoln.

Don drives home on automatic pilot. It is like the route from the Grove Park to Sunset Parkway is just another synapse in his brain. Carrie scoots over on the bench seat and leans against him, with her left hand on his right thigh. "I hope you're not sleepy," she says.

As he pulls into his driveway, he sees a red convertible pull away from the house next door. That's not too unusual, as the secluded loop is a favorite place for high schoolers to go parking.

Don unlocks the kitchen door, and Carrie enters to find Becky sipping a glass of milk and nibbling on a graham cracker.

"How was he?" she asks Becky.

"Perfect, as usual. We played Scrabble, and I don't know how he got such a good vocabulary. He spelled 'quivers' and got 19 points. He's still ten, right?"

"Turns 11 in three months, on January 15."

"Well, he's one smart little dude. And he went straight to bed at nine. No fuss. Never is with him. I just came down from checking on him and he was snoozing away."

"Can I walk you home?" Don asks.

"Sure. Thanks."

"Oh, wait," Carrie says. "How could I forget? Here's your twenty. Can you do next Saturday?"

"Thanks. I'll check and call you. Bye! And have a wonderful evening!"

Don and Becky exit the front door, while Carrie opens the cupboard for the aspirin bottle.

She downs three tablets and then realizes she has to pee. In the downstairs half-bath, she studies herself in the mirror. In the glare of the light, her buzz starts to fade, and she worries that she's already 35 and not getting younger. Her thoughts jumble together.

What am I waiting for? All I need is just a little fun every now and then, and I don't mean a fancy Grove Park ball, which I figure cost us $20,000 per dance. But that's for tomorrow. For now, go up and check on my little prince, then I'll surprise Don.

Carrie's ascent upstairs is softened by the newly carpeted stairs. She thinks it is unusual that Becky would close Matthew's door. As she opens it, a whoosh of cool fall air flows through the room. Carrie does not notice Billy's note, which blew off the table and landed under the bed. She tiptoes over and sees the bed empty. Maybe he's in the bathroom? But his door was shut. He must be trying to trick her. "Come out, Matthew. I know you're in here. It's late, and you have Sunday School then you're reading at worship."

Carrie turns on the ceiling light. She looks in the closet. She looks under the bed, but still does not see the note. She finds his teddy on the floor. Clutching it, she looks out the window and sees the ladder. A flash goes off in her head, like a white sheet on the line snapping in the sun and momentarily blinding her. Her spine tingles.

"Matthew!" She calls out to the neighborhood. "*Matthew*, come here! You're *scaring* me!"

No response, except for the rustling of the leaves, a few of which are fluttering down.

She backs away from the window. This is way too much.

She shrieks, "*He's run away! Matthew!*"

Don hears the leaf-filtered screams from a block away as he walks back to the house. They grow clearer and louder with each step. When he is two houses away, he is stunned by the realization that they are coming from his house and that the person screaming is his wife.

He runs in the front door and finds Carrie blown-out on the bottom step. Her mascara is all smeared and her coiffed hair is sticking out at the wrong places. She cradles the teddy bear next to her chest like it is her beating heart.

"What in *God's* name is going on?" Don demands.

Carrie looks up at him but can hardly get a word out of her swollen throat.

Then slowly, like each word is a stone, "He's *gone*. He ran away. There's a ladder."

Confused, Don runs up the steps to see for himself. He is quickly outside at the base of the ladder. He looks up and sees socks on the top rails of the ladder but can't make sense of it. He looks around the yard for something, anything, that would help him understand. He sees no clues.

Why would Matthew run away? He was fine, wasn't he? Don tries to remember all of Saturday—the burger and fries at Hardee's (the usual), the Reds-Pirates game (he was upbeat), the picture-taking (he was ok), the hug with Becky (which he'd been doing for years).

Don walks back in as Carrie is pulling herself up and together. "I'm calling the police," she says matter-of-factly as she starts for the kitchen.

"No. Not yet. Let's give it a little bit. This may be just an adventure around the neighborhood. Paul could have cooked this up and maybe Matthew went along. Like a Tom Sawyer thing. He's a good boy. He'll be back soon."

"You don't know that. Please, Don, we have to *do* something!"

"Just give it a little bit. If the police know, then the papers will know, then our friends will know. What are they going to think—that we're bad parents? That Matthew is an unhappy child? That kind of stuff doesn't go away for a long time. Let's give it an hour."

Carrie, exhausted, slumps into the den sofa, the one recently occupied by Becky and her boyfriend. She sees that Becky forgot her calculus book.

Don paces, then sits helplessly beside her and holds her. He remembers that a red convertible was leaving as he and Carrie were arriving.

"You stay here while I go back out. I'm going to cruise around the neighborhood and will be back in less than 20 minutes. You ok? Can you stay here in case he comes back?"

"*Am I ok?* Our son is *gone* and you ask if I'm *ok*?" Carrie's face is flush and contorted.

Don remembers the black days from over ten years ago and wants to shout: Carrie, dammit, keep it together, don't slip back into the hellhole.

The hellhole was a year after they married. They had driven to Charlotte for a weekend. On Saturday morning, at the Mint Museum, while they were casually walking alongside the walls of paintings, Carrie started to talk nonsense, not just to Don but to the walls. She asked Don if he could hear voices.

"What voices?"

"The ones behind the walls."

"Stop acting crazy."

Carrie walked right up to an oil of Edward Hopper and rubbed her finger on it.

"Don't touch the painting!" A guard barked.

Don could not make out what was going on, which was Carrie tipping over and into the vortex and quickly spiraling down.

She sat on a bench and started pulling at her hair.

"Sweetie! What's wrong?"

As Don found out that afternoon at the emergency room, Carrie had until then successfully kept from him her secret. Ever since she started college, she had been on anti-depressants. She never told Don because she was ashamed. In the rush to leave Asheville, she had forgotten her pill box.

And now here she was being sedated.

On Sunday Don drove in the bewilderment of Carrie having kept him in the dark. He vacillated between being angry and sympathetic. He wanted to say how could you have not told me, but instead said I love you, no matter what. Carrie's response was word salad, as the doctor in Charlotte called it. Part of it was "afraid" and "you leaving me."

The next weeks were brutal. Carrie kept hearing voices from no one. She accused Don of cheating on her and even described what the other woman was wearing. When she would calm down, she had this flat look on her face. Don kept it all inside and hoped this would be short-lived, so that people didn't have to know. No one knew except for them and the psychiatrist she saw in private sessions for two months.

She recovered. Things got better. Cards were on the table. They got pregnant and had Matthew, and things were as normal as they could get, with the nightly pill that Don made sure she took.

Carrie is still on the sofa when Don says, "It'll be all right. Try to calm down. I'll be right back."

Carrie's headache is like a hatchet pressing down against the top of her head. She sits on the front steps with her head propped in her hands. "Mommy?" she thinks she hears. She scans the yard and the bushes. "Mommy?"

"Matthew! Come out! This isn't funny!"

———————

Skin almost gets car sick while Billy drives south on the winding US 74 to a point just beyond Bat Cave on the way to Chimney Rock. He slows and steers the Impala off the paved road onto a gravel one that he and Skin know well from deer hunting. It's not gun season yet, so he figures, rightly, that no one will be here.

He drives a half mile zigzagging up to the dead end and backs in. Neither he nor Skin has said a word to each other since they left Willie's. Both, however, heard the boy bumping around as Billy took the turns faster than he should have. After he kills the motor, Billy says, "Let's see what we got." He and Skin open the trunk and turn the flashlight on Matthew.

"Ah, shit. He's peed all over himself!" Billy says with disgust.

"What'd you expect? You would too. Anyone would. Now let's get him out."

Matthew is curled and frozen. It takes a while for them to lift him out and put the rope around his neck. He is still gagged, blindfolded, and bound with duct tape. Shining him with the flashlight, they can see he's having some sort of allergic reaction to the tape around his mouth and eyes.

They have to get the boy to walk. Carrying him to the cave is not possible.

"Listen," Billy whispers into the boy's ear, trying to sound reassuring, "you cooperate and you don't get hurt. We're not going to hurt you unless you try to run away or do something stupid. We just want your old man to give us some dough, and then we give you back. Should just take a day or two. You understand?"

Matthew is shaking with fear. He remembers the gun and thinks he is about to die. But he manages to utter a sound that Billy takes as a yes.

Skin looks closer at Matthew with the light and is concerned for the boy. He talks to Billy using the fake name they agreed on.

"Hey Jim, he's got some problem with the tape on his head, and we don't need another problem. Can we just cut the tape off and use the stocking for a mask?"

Billy is ok with that, and it is quickly done in the dark, with Matthew facing away from them. Then they set off on the trail with Billy holding the leash and the flashlight and Skin carrying their stash of essentials: weed, booze, water, food, and blankets.

The going is slow, because all three of them, mostly Matthew, trip over tree roots and slide in the leafy ooze of the mountain.

———

Don is back and he leads Carrie in from the front steps.

"*Do* something, Don!"

"Ok, I'll call. Come what may."

He dials 9-1-1 for the first time in his life.

"This is Don Harwood. I live at 46 Sunset Parkway. My ten-year old son is missing, as of about an hour ago. There was a ladder next to his bedroom window.... "

"Mr. Harwood, stay where you are. I'll contact the police dispatcher and we'll have officers there as soon as we can. Can you describe the appearance of the boy?"

"He's about four-and-a-half feet tall. Blond hair—a little longish and curly. Blue eyes. Probably in his pajamas, unless he changed."

Within ten minutes, the police car pulls up. Don thanks God they don't have their lights or siren on. He is waiting for them on the sidewalk. He first shows them the ladder, then takes them to Matthew's room.

Officer Number One interviews Don and Carrie about Matthew's history, state of mind, friends, enemies, teachers, coaches, favorite subjects, hobbies, until they can't think straight.

Don and Carrie take turns describing their son and his life. They show the officers Matthew's sketch pad, which contains pencil and pen-and-ink drawings made by a precocious boy observing his world with an sharpness beyond his years. There is a drawing of three apples that seem round enough to pick up from the paper and bite into.

"Anything unusual recently?" Number One asks them.

Don's and Carrie's minds are swirling sickly like they just got off a roller coaster. "There was a car, a red convertible. It was driving off next door as we were coming in. I haven't seen it before."

"Matthew's door was closed when I came up," Carrie is thinking more clearly now. "He always leaves it open. So does Becky, our babysitter. And he left his glasses."

"The ladder...." Don starts to connect the dots, "the ladder may be from next door. The Reids moved out while they fix up their house, and there have been crews there every day. But not on weekends."

"Oh," Carrie remembers, "Becky said she had just come down from checking on him right before we arrived... wouldn't she have seen he wasn't here?"

"So she would have been the last one to see him?" Officer Number One asks.

"Of course," Carrie responds.

"When I walked her home, there didn't seem to be any problem." Don says with a puzzled look.

Officer Number One says, "We need to get her back over here now."

Number Two is looking carefully in the closet and around the room.

Two asks Carrie to come to the closet. "Are these all of his shoes and sneakers? Any missing?"

Carrie counts. "That's all of them. Look: those are his favorite Adidas. He would have worn them to go outside. What's going on?"

Number Two asks if anything has been disturbed in the room, and Carrie says no. On the top of his dresser, his collection of a rabbit's foot, an arrowhead, and a small Swiss Army knife are all in place. She says she took his teddy bear, which had fallen to the floor.

The officer crawls on the floor and points his flashlight under the bed. He sees Billy's note and pinches the edge of it so as not to contaminate any evidence. He pulls it out into the light and starts to read to himself.

"Jesus Christ" is all he can say.

They all crouch around to see for themselves:

"Call the babysitter and get her over here at once" Number One instructs Don and Carrie. Then to his partner, "You better call Detective Laney right now."

Carrie uses the upstairs phone. "Becky, Matthew is missing. There was a ladder under his window. The police are here. They need to ask you some questions. Now."

Becky is shocked. She tells herself it must be a misunderstanding. Then she tells her parents, she has to, and they go with her to the Harwoods.

Officer Number One sits them down in the den, while Number Two takes his flashlight outside.

"Mrs. Harwood said they got home around 10:45, and you told them you had just checked on their son," the policeman said to Becky. "She says that, within a couple of minutes, she discovered the boy's not here. So, did you check on him sometime around 10:30, and was he there?"

Becky's head is humming so loudly she can hardly think. She sees her calculus book on the floor. She is sitting with her parents on the same sofa on which she and her boyfriend were messing around, just an hour ago.

"I didn't check on him," Becky finally says, so low no one can hear her.

"You need to speak up, young lady," One says.

"I didn't check on him. Woody, my boyfriend, was over here, and we were watching TV right here. Then he left. Then you came in."

"*Becky!*" Both of her parents exclaim in unison. "Becky, how *could* you?"

"I'm sorry. There's never been any problem with Matt-Matt. He goes up when I say it's time, he turns his lights out, and that's it. There's nothing else for me to do."

"And now he's gone!" Don shouts, startling everyone, including himself.

"I'm so sorry. I didn't hear anything. What can I do?" Becky pleads.

Officer One, who is taking notes, says, "You can start by giving us Woody's full name and phone number. And tell us what kind of car he drives."

The trek up the trail is especially tedious because it heads almost straight up the mountain side and then follows a rocky ridge—at some places there is a sheer, straight drop-off of over 200 feet. Billy, Skin, and Matthew reach the cave after about 20 minutes of slushing and slipping. By now, it's almost midnight. All three are drop-dead exhausted. The moon is on the other side of the earth, and there is no nearby light reflected by the clouds. The surrounding mountains look like the haunches of slumbering black bears.

Billy believes that hundreds of years ago Cherokee hunters used to hole up in this cave for its view of the valley. It looks like a gaping jaw in the side of the mountain, but its floor is relatively flat and extends back about 15 feet. The only cause for complaint is how dank the place is, from water constantly dripping off the ceiling.

Skin spreads out the blankets. He and Billy have a night cap, each taking a healthy slug out of a pint bottle. Skin thinks about rolling a joint but decides he'd rather crash.

Billy tells him, "Give the boy some water. Need to keep him in good shape."

Skin pulls the stretchy nylon aside and pours some water in Matthew's mouth. The boy almost chokes on it. The second try works better.

Skin whispers to him, "It's going to be ok, kid." Then, not appreciating the irony, he says, "good night."

Skin puts Matthew on a blanket and wraps him in the excess material. Billy ties the leash around his ankle so he'll know if Matthew tries to get up.

Involuntarily, Matthew recites to himself Psalms 23, which he had memorized for tomorrow's service at First Baptist:

> *The Lord is my shepherd;*
> *I shall not want...*
> *Yea, though I walk through*
> *the valley of the shadow*

of death, I will fear no evil;
For Thou art with me;
Thy rod and Thy staff,
They comfort me…
Surely goodness and mercy shall follow me all the days of my life;
And I will dwell in the house of the Lord Forever.

He closes his blue eyes behind the black blindfold. A solitary tear is absorbed by the nylon. He starts the verse again, but before he gets to "leadeth me in the paths…," he falls fast asleep.

———

SUNDAY   The two officers, Charlie and Trip, wake with the dawn light and the smell of coffee that Carrie is brewing. Don and Carrie have not slept a wink.

The dynamic is surreal. Matthew is gone. The officers are in the kitchen. Everyone is groggy with the lack of sleep and overwhelmed with worry and tension. Don is unusually grumpy. So when Carrie tells Don once again to *do* something, he snaps in turn at the policemen: "Why don't *you* people *do* something?"

"We are doing something," Trip says calmly. "First, we are staying here until you get the call. Second, we have every available man cruising around Asheville for any sign of Matthew. And third, Detective Laney is making an early morning visit to Woody to ask him some tough questions and to check out his car. I know it's hard, but we've just got to wait this out."

Don hears the clunk of the Sunday paper hitting the driveway. He starts to fetch it but turns to the policemen instead: "You haven't told the papers anything, have you?"

"No," says Charlie. "That's not going to help things until we see what the kidnappers say. Sooner or later, though, the papers are going to find out, and you'll need to make them your friends."

The house is eerily quiet, with just the percolator popping, as Don turns to get the paper.

Ring, ring, ring—the phone startles the bejesus out of everyone. They didn't think it would come so early. Carrie knocks her coffee cup over on the table as she starts to rise, but Don is the first to the phone. He answers, "Hello?"

It's just Detective Laney, who reports that Woody was scared shitless when Laney banged on the dorm room door at 6:00 a.m. at UNC-Asheville. But Woody cooperated and is clean, with no leads to chase. He can be scratched off the list of suspects.

———

Matthew can tell it is getting light even through the black nylon. It is perfectly still and quiet, except for the birds calling and the two men breathing heavily. Matthew stays still and quiet, too, until the awful weight of his situation presses down on him. This may be his last day, he thinks. They may kill him. How would they do it? They said if he did what they said, he wouldn't get hurt, but he didn't believe them. What are Mommy and Daddy doing?

Matthew cannot see that it is a brilliant, God-made Sunday morning in the mountains of Western North Carolina, where under the bluebird sky the leaves are just beginning their turn from lush green to crisp yellow and red. From the vantage point of the cave, it looks like a coat of many colors cast over the rolling valley.

Without sight, Matthew's other senses magnify. He smells the slightly pungent turpentine of the white pine needles that surround the cave's entrance and remembers a Saturday in late August, before school started. He tries to focus on it to escape the present.

He and his dad pick up Paul and his dad at 6:00 in the morning. Matthew and Paul sleep in the back seat and wake up at the Exxon station when they get off I-40 west of Asheville at Wilton Springs to use the restroom and for the dads to refuel with coffee. The boys split a pack of powdered doughnuts and laugh at their white lips. Then they drive on the two-lane that borders the northern side of the Great Smoky Mountains National Park, pass straight through an awakening Gatlinburg, and turn left onto Nature Trails Road. Within a half hour they park at the trailhead, puddled from yesterday's rain, and unload four small backpacks and two walking sticks for the dads. Matthew looks at one of the puddles and sees the reflection of clouds sailing overhead.

The boys lace up their Adidas, and the dads use their fingers as shoehorns for new hiking boots. They say good morning to a couple who is assembling their gear and donning floppy hats.

Then they are off, fresh in the cool morning mountain air and seeing their breath, starting up Rainbow Falls Trail on an ambitious adventure all the way to Mount Le Conte, over six miles up. With a pact not to stop until they are at the top, they follow Le Conte Creek to the falls and switchback up, back and forth and back and forth, seemingly endlessly until they finally reach the summit. They are 6,500 feet above sea level, on top of the world, with a panoramic view that leaves them breathless from exhaustion and the glory of it.

Matthew and Paul perch on the rocks, with their dads saying, "stop, don't go out any farther, it's a long way down if you fall." A fellow hiker obliges their request and snaps a picture of them smiling in front of the blue, distant mountains. Then they find a flat rock and picnic in the sun on peanut butter and jelly, chips, almond Hershey bars, and Cokes from the lodge.

The way down, of course, is easy, but still with seemingly endless switchbacks. The boys have unbounded energy, a product of youth, chocolate, and caffeine, and the dads lag behind occasionally talking about sports. Matthew and Paul literally skip along and hear a refrain of "wait up" whenever they get out of sight.

The boys alternate taking the lead, playfully pushing past each other, bumping shoulders. Matthew has just landed a good body check on Paul before looking straight ahead and seeing two black bear cubs in the middle of the trail, about 40 feet ahead. He and Paul stop in their tracks, as do the cubs, each side eyeing the other.

When the dads catch up, the mama bear is moving onto the trail between the cubs and the hikers. She starts to growl and swats the ground with her catcher's-mitt-size paw. She takes a step toward the boys and stops. She starts to rear up and stops. The staring game goes on until Don says, remarkably calmly, "Remember, we read the sign at the trailhead about this. Everybody raise your hands and shout and then jump right, through the woods, to the switchback below.... Ready? Go!"

The mama bear looks on curiously as the four of them yell, "Ahhhhh!" and quickly disappear down a steep slope. The boys slide and the dads do their best to stay afoot, running through a thicket of rhododendron and teaberry and roots of elms.

Paul's dad screams again. The others turn back to see him on the ground, head downhill, with a boot caught in a tangle of roots.

"Stay here." Don tells the boys. He climbs back up, releases the boot from the roots, and helps Paul's dad move gingerly down to the trail.

"It's my ankle. I twisted it. Let's keep going or it'll swell."

Don lends his walking stick, and Paul's dad limps downhill. The group of four stays close together.

At Rainbow Falls, they stop, as planned, and Paul's dad soaks his bare, bluing ankle in the cold water. Meanwhile, Don teaches Matthew and Paul how to skip stones by finding flat ones and throwing them side-armed so that they spin horizontally above the surface and then hop three or four times if they're lucky before succumbing to gravity and sinking. After exhausting the collection of good stones on the bank, the boys take off their shoes, socks, and shirts and wade in the shallows to a dry, sun-warmed, table rock, where they stretch out for five minutes before they become restless. They sit up, then stand and start to climb the mist- and algae-slippery rocks in the pool. Matthew beats his chest and does a Tarzan yell. He turns to look at his dad. Don reaches for his backpack to get the camera, but before he can hold it up Matthew slips and slides feet first underwater. He sinks as quickly as a rock. Then he pops up and shivers, with his arms flailing. Before Don gets to him, Matthew pulls himself upright and pulls Paul in off the rock, the two of them oblivious to the cold. As Don drags himself out back to the shore, the boys swim over and let the waterfall pound their heads.

Fortunately, thanks to Carrie's foresight, they have towels and a change of clothes in the car.

On the ride back, both boys fall dead asleep with half-eaten, Gatlin-burg-made taffy on their laps.

Matthew's trance-like day dream is interrupted by a sudden, strong need to pee. He rolls over to try and get up, and the rope yanks where it's attached to Billy's ankle and tightens around Matthew's neck, which is getting raw in places. Billy sits up with a start and grabs his pistol.

Matthew tries to say "bathroom" through his gag, but it comes out as "*un-um.*"

By this time, Skin is awake and says, "He's got to pee."

"Shit, at this hour?" Billy grunts. "You take him out," said like Matthew was a dog that needed relief. Billy undoes the rope from his ankle, and Skin leads Matthew into the woods.

Skin holds the leash, but Matthew just stands there.

"Oh, sorry," says Skin. "Forgot you can't use your hands. Oh, well."

Skin pulls the pajama bottoms down, feeling a little embarrassed.

Matthew goes for a long time. Then Skin fixes him up and they return to the cave, where Billy is sitting cross-legged and scowling.

After some negotiation, with Skin arguing that they have to treat the kid decent, he and Billy agree to remove the gag in order to give Matthew some breakfast. Billy lectures Matthew that if he utters a sound he'll regret it, like maybe he'll never see his Mommy and Daddy again.

Skin unties the nylon gag, gives Matthew water, and then shares some beef jerky, which tastes like the sweaty leather of a baseball glove. Then he is re-gagged.

Afterwards, Billy says it's time for him to make the call.

"I'm coming with you," says Skin.

"The hell you are! You have to guard our prize possession."

"How am I gonna know what you say to them? Besides, the kid ain't going nowhere."

"Trust me, Skin. I can't do nothing without you and the boy. Just sit tight. And don't get too friendly."

Then Billy walks off down the trail, saying he'll be back in an hour or so.

Skin sits, then leans back on the pine needles.

"We're going to need everything you have on your son," Charlie breaks the silence of the foursome who sit and wait at 46 Sunset Parkway. "Medical records, dental records, list of teachers, list of friends. Did he go to any camps? Can you think of anything else, Detective?"

Detective Laney, who replaced Trip at the scene, asks Don and Carrie, "Do you know of anyone who you might have ticked off? Anything that might have turned someone against you? This may not be just about money."

They shake their heads.

Unlike the officers, Laney is not in uniform. He wears a sports jacket and a narrow tie with a silver clip that slides into his shirt. Ever since his tour of duty in Korea, he has kept his crew cut and is a fit and sinewy man. Even though he pinches a lit Camel between his thumb and forefinger, he looks like he could run a marathon without any training. He is also somewhat gruff, and Don and Carrie are put off at first with his apparent lack of sympathy.

Once again, the phone rings like a screeching nerve and scares everyone to death.

Don answers, "Hello?"

The voice on the other end is difficult to hear. Billy, calling from inside the pay phone booth outside the Old Cider Mill in Bat Cave, is tapping a beer can against the glass in order to disguise his voice.

"Don Harwood?" Billy asks between the racket.

"Yes? Who's this?"

"We got your boy. If you want to see him alive again, I need you to get a suitcase full of twenties, $100,000 worth, by 2:00 tomorrow afternoon. Once we're sure it's all there, we release him. Do you understand me?"

"Yes. But I can't get that kind of money by tomorrow. And I need to know my son is ok."

"Mister, I think you'd best remember that *I'm* the one who's telling *you* what to do. You can take it or leave it. I'll call tomorrow with the drop-off place."

Click.

Don's hand shakes as he returns the receiver.

He repeats what he could make out verbatim to Carrie, Charlie, and Laney.

Laney asks if Don could tell where the caller was, and Don says it sounded like he was in a factory with some kind of machinery close by.

"Did you recognize the voice? Is it anyone you know?" Laney asks while stubbing out his cigarette.

"No. I don't think it's anybody I know. But it was hard to hear with all the racket."

Don drops into a kitchen chair and puts his face in his hands and tries to see beyond the void.

While Billy is away for the call, Skin holds the leash, even though he knows that if he let go Matthew wouldn't bolt blindly into the woods.

The time passes slowly, and eventually Matthew falls back asleep, worn down from the constant terror. Skin feels comfortable enough to let go of the rope while he goes out to relieve himself. Then he rolls a couple of joints for when Billy gets back and he lies next to Matthew just outside the cave under the robin-egg sky of autumn. The sun shines down with a clarity reserved for autumn. It illuminates the golden head of Matthew, which seems to glow as a lesser sun.

Skin picks a pine needle out of Matthew's blond hair. Skin starts to talk himself out of this. He could walk Matthew out and both of them could catch a ride at the road. Then Skin could skedaddle out of North Carolina to . . . to somewhere else and start over. Just then, he hears Billy huffing back up the trail, and it's too late. But he tells himself it's going to be up to him to protect Matthew until they can get their dough and be done with this. The kid didn't do anything to deserve this.

Night falls around the cave. The three of them sit around the abandoned fire pit, which they don't use for obvious reasons. With his pocket knife, Skin opens a can of pork-and-beans. Billy finishes the last of their appetizer, Fritos. He holds a sleeve of saltines, waiting to dip them in the can.

"Just think of it," Billy sounds softer than usual, almost dreamy. "This is our last night of a poor man's meal. From tomorrow on, it's nothing but steaks. Hell, we could buy a whole steak restaurant."

"Let's hope Don comes through," Skin says.

Hearing his father's name, Matthew thinks of his parents in the kitchen, not knowing what happened to him. He wants to walk in the door and say I'm back.

"Why wouldn't he?" Billy is confident. "He's got to get Goldilocks back safe and sound."

Skin needs to detach. He rolled two joints, and it seems to him fitting that they should smoke them. Why wait? There's more stashed at the trailer park.

Midway into the first one, Billy gets giddy with his bright future, and he begins to hum and sing the Bob Dylan song about ride me high and we gonna fly.

Skin stays quiet. He guesses Billy forgot that the name of that song is "You Ain't Goin' Nowhere."

After the joints are gone and stubbed out, Billy and Skin clink their respective pints of whiskey together. Each bottle is three-quarters full and soon to be drained.

Meanwhile, Skin pulls Matthew's gag down and gives him water, followed by the last cracker and the residue of the pork-and-beans. Something goes down the wrong pipe again, and Matthew starts to cough and wheeze. This irritates Billy, who thinks his authority is being challenged. He grabs Skin's pocket knife, pushes the boy over on his side, and holds the knife to his throat, drawing a drop of blood. "Listen to me, you little son of a bitch, I said no noise. So shut up!"

"Hey! Come on! Put that down!" Skin pulls back at Billy's shoulder.

Billy pushes the boy hard and away. Then he stands up, dusts off, tosses the knife onto Skin's lap, and walks into the woods to relieve himself. While Billy's gone, Skin reassures Matthew, "This time tomorrow, you'll be home in your nice fluffy bed."

Matthew doesn't trust or believe him, but at least he's better than the other one. He curls up on his blanket. He trembles, tells himself to relax, and ultimately falls asleep.

Billy and Skin make up while they talk of Florida, sun, and the prospect of bikini-clad women on the beach. They sip the last drops of liquor. Within a half hour, they are both slurring, numb, and oblivious.

Skin passes out cold. Billy tries to tie the rope around his ankle, but his thick fingers can't get the loop right.

"There," he says, thinking he has secured a knot.

After the ransom call, Don spends most of his Sunday tracking down the presidents of the three biggest banks in Asheville. He knows all of them personally from the Rotary Club and the country club, and all three banks are asset-backed lenders to Quality Furniture. One of the banks holds the mortgage on the Harwoods' home.

He asks each of them to come to his home at 4:00 p.m. He tells them that this is a personal emergency and that he needs their immediate help. When they ask what's up, he cuts off the conversation and says it's better to discuss face-to-face in private.

Each of them thinks this is a one-on-one invitation and is surprised to see others pull up in front of the house at the same time.

"Well," National says to State and Community, "it's always nice to see you fellas, but what are you doing here?"

"I have no earthly idea," says Community, "Guess we'll all find out together."

Community thinks Don should have given him a clue. After all, he was

Don's fraternity brother at Wofford. In their junior year, 1957, he had introduced Don to Carrie.

All three bankers are equally clueless as they are ushered into the living room by Carrie. They all sit awkwardly on the sofa, and Carrie wishes again that she'd had it reupholstered.

Don walks in and shakes their hands while thanking them for coming. Then he sits opposite them in an armchair. Carrie stands behind him with her hands on his shoulders.

Don begins, "I'm sorry to drag you all here like this, but it's about our son Matthew. He's gone." He cannot continue because, for the first time since Saturday night, his whole soul rises up through his constricted throat, and he heaves uncontrollably with sobs. Carrie stands as silent as a statue.

"Oh my God, Don, I didn't even know he was sick, or was it an accident?" Community offers.

"I'm so sorry," say National and State together.

Don's episode dies down, and he stares at the Oriental rug for 20 counted seconds trying to regain his composure and his ability to speak.

With a raspy voice, he continues: "It's not that. He was kidnapped—*kidnapped!*—last night from his bedroom window when Carrie and I were at the Grove Park."

"Jesus!" says National.

"Holy shit!" says State.

"They called me today and demanded $100,000 in twenties. By two tomorrow afternoon."

"In twenties?" State says. "That's . . . 5,000 bills!"

"The detective they put on the case is keeping this out of the press for now, so you have to keep this under wraps," Don says. "He also advises that we should not pay the ransom, that doing so would only encourage them to ask for more or do this to somebody else. Right now, to be honest, I don't care about any of that. I—we—want Matthew back tomorrow. Can you imagine what he's going through?"

"I can't imagine what you two are going through," Community says. "I'm having a hard time comprehending any of this."

"Look," Don gets firm and urgent. "I've been a good customer, and I am good for the money. I'll sign a note, I'll do whatever you need me to. But I need 5,000 twenties by noon tomorrow."

"This won't be easy," National says, "tomorrow's Columbus Day. We're closed."

"Jesus," Don says. "Surely you can get into your own banks on Columbus Day."

The threesome caucuses, and State reports: "Ok. Of course, ok. We'll do 35-35-30. When do you need it?"

"Here, by noon tomorrow. Thank you so much. I knew you'd come through. And now, if you'll excuse me, I'm going to have a shot of Scotch and try to get some rest."

Don gets up and shakes hands again. "I won't forget this," he says as he walks away with Carrie, leaving the bankers to show themselves out.

———

Don and Carrie try to rest, but it's no use. They lay side-by-side on their queen size and take turns rolling from one shoulder to the other. Don thinks about another Scotch. Carrie, now on her back and staring at the ceiling, says they should call Dr. Porter, the Senior Pastor at First Baptist Church. She is the more devout one of the two because she thinks it keeps her glued together. Don agrees as a way to help her cope, as long as Dr. Porter promises to keep it all to himself. So she calls, and he agrees to come and be discreet, and they put their clothes back on.

As they show Dr. Porter into the living room, Don has the out-of-body feeling that this can't be happening to him. It was just yesterday afternoon when he and Matthew were watching the game, and it suddenly occurs to him that game 2 is now history as well. He doesn't care who won.

Not sounding like her normal voice, Carrie tells her pastor that Matthew has been kidnapped and that there is a ransom demand.

"Jesus Christ!" Dr. Porter doesn't acknowledge that his reaction wasn't befitting of his stature. Instead, he does what he does best.

He kneels on the rug and spreads his arms. "Pray with me," he beseeches. It comes out more like a command than a request.

Awkwardly, Don and Carrie kneel, and they hold hands in a circle as the pastor begins:

"Gracious God, the Glorious One who gave his only begotten Son to be crucified, dead, and buried, only to rise on the third day, be with us now. Bless Don and Carrie, and bless their only son Matthew, wherever he may be, and protect him from those that would do him bodily harm."

The pastor drones on until Carrie coughs. Then he sums up: "In the name of our Lord and Savior Jesus Christ, Amen."

Don and Carrie are obliged to say, "Amen."

Don is quick to thank the pastor for coming and to close the door behind him.

"To be honest, I feel worse now," he confides to Carrie.

"I'm sorry I asked him. I just felt so alone. And maybe Matthew can hear our prayer."

Don silently agrees with her, though that prayer does not need to be spoken. It permeates their entire souls; they breathe it with every breath and taste it bitterly on their tongues. It is the prayer of a mother and father that their stolen child is nearby, safe, and soon to be returned to them. It is a prayer that they will relinquish anything, even their own lives, for his. It is a prayer that they hope will dampen their smoldering fear and anger, as if a prayer could do such a thing.

———————

MONDAY   In the darkness, from high in a white pine directly overhead, a great horned owl calls out: *Hoo-hoo, hoo-hoo, hoo-hoo ....*

The haunting, repetitive sound stirs Matthew from his sleep. He rolls over from his left side to his right and stretches out, moving his shoulders and head away from Billy. Suddenly, he realizes he is free of the bond, able to move his legs freely. His eyes pop open behind the black blindfold. An inch at a time, he slides farther away from the unconscious Billy.

It dawns on him that he has a choice. If he stays put and cooperates, he may get traded back to his parents and be home today—*if* the men keep their word. He thinks of the man with the black stocking mask pointing a gun at him, breathing foul air, calling him bad names, and threatening to kill him. He's ok with the other one, whom he's never seen, but the friendlier one is not calling the shots.

Hoo-hoo, hoo-hoo, hoo-hoo....

Or he can leave. He remembers through the feelings in his feet from when he was brought to the cave: going down would be a slippery trail with roots, a gravel road, a paved road.

He doesn't have much time before the men wake up, especially with the owl hooting.

Does he trust them or himself?

He pinches his face up behind the blindfold and gag, and blood rushes to his head, which begins to pulse with resolve.

With his hands bound behind him, getting up is difficult. He lies on his side and curls up. Then he faces down. With all his strength, and with his forehead mashing into the pine needles, he manages to prop up on his knees. Then he puts his left foot down, then his right, and finally he is standing. He wobbles a bit, but he is standing.

Skin's dream is interrupted by nearby sounds that he can't make out. He props up on his elbows at the prospect of a bear or wildcat and feels his head pound. He's still half-drunk. He looks right and sees Matthew standing a couple of yards away from Billy.

Skin opens his mouth to say, "Wait!" But nothing comes out. Instead, he thinks the kid doesn't deserve this, and who's to say Don will come through with the cash anyway?

Slowly, Matthew takes his first step toward what he hopes is the trail home.

Skin's eye twitches as he watches Matthew. He starts to jab Billy awake but something stops him, and he lies back down. He falls back asleep.

It is not too long before Matthew bumps into the sharp stub of a limb protruding from the trunk of an old oak tree. It scratches his cheek, and he recoils. Then he carefully moves forward again, this time finding the branch intentionally. He rubs the back of his head against it, up and down and up and down, until, several precious minutes later, he manages to use it to pull the blindfold off his head. It is the first time he has been able to see since Saturday night in his bedroom. Or at least it would be, but it is as dark as death, he doesn't have his glasses, and he can make out only a few indistinct objects. He thinks he sees the path and takes another step.

———————

Don and Carrie are up early. They stand together at the threshold of Matthew's room and wonder what the day will bring.

Carrie figures she might as well say it or it will explode inside her. "How long has it been since I asked you to replace the screen on his window?"

Don avoids her eyes, which he can feel burning into the side of his head. He wants to say, "So now it's my fault that some criminal stole our son?" But he thinks better of it, he always does, and simply turns away, heading downstairs. The last thing they need now is a fight.

Carrie stays to make up Matthew's bed and put his teddy bear back where it belongs, sitting against the pillow.

They mechanically work together making toast and frying eggs and percolating coffee, busy work that fails to distract them from staring at the phone, as if looking at it would cause it to ring and start the process of getting all of this horror over with. It does not ring. And they do not eat, just push their plates aside.

Next door at the Reid's house, Detective Laney and Charlie show their badges as they greet the arriving construction foreman and the workers. The interrogations are one-on-one. A painter gives hesitant, somewhat inconsistent answers to what he was doing Saturday night, and Charlie takes him to the station for further questioning.

At the cave, Billy snorts and rolls to his side. Skin opens his left eye to the spinning daylight. He sits up and opens his other eye to see how the boy's doing, having forgotten for a moment seeing Matthew walk off.

He sees an empty spot where the boy should be. Skin rubs the sleepers out of his eyes and opens them wide to see better. He has a dark, diving feeling he has fucked up royally.

"*Billy!*" He pushes hard on his friend's arm.

"What the fu...?" Billy grunts.

"*Billy! The boy is gone!*"

Billy bolts upright and reaches for the pistol. He turns his stiff neck side to side to take account of the campsite.

"Shee-it. Can't be far. May be peeing. You go right and I'll go left. Meet back here in five."

After five minutes of stumbling through the woods, they return and stare at each other with open palms, both looking confused.

"*God dammit to hell!*" Billy yells. "How the *fuck* could he not be here? He's blindfolded, for God's sake! Unless... unless... *you* took it off?"

"No way, dude. No way. I'm in this for the dough."

"But you were getting soft on him, weren't you?" Billy shoves Skin.

"Look, Billy," Skin tries to look right at Billy but his eye twitches. "You and I conked out last night at the same time. We woke up at the same time. You were supposed to have him tied to your ankle. So I don't know what happened, but I didn't do anything." The inside of Skin's head is whirling around.

Billy tries to suppress his anger so that he can focus on this more clearly. He sits down and combs his hand through his hair.

"All right," he says, "let's think. First we get our shit and get out of here. If we see the boy on the way out, we're back in the game. If we don't see him, well, shit, I guess we get our butts to QF before 8:30 so nobody thinks it's us."

"Ain't this supposed to be a holiday?"

"Not for QF. Not for us."

"Why can't we just collect the dough and skip town and be done with it?"

"They're not idiots. They'll want to see him or hear him on the phone or something before they make the delivery. And this is just *spooking* me now, ok? I am so fucking *spooked* I can't stand it. How could the kid untie the knot when his hands are tied up? You... ? Ah, fuck it. We gotta go quick. Keep your eyes open on the way down, can you at least do that?"

By 11:00, each of three bank presidents call Don and say more or less the same thing: they have the cash, and he can pick it up downtown and sign a promissory note in front of a notary public. Each call sends Don through the roof, first because he thinks it is the kidnappers calling to arrange the exchange, and second because he gets more irritated each time that the bankers don't realize he cannot leave the house.

So National, State, and Community each come by with their delivery, and Don signs papers that he does not read. By noon, $100,000 is stacked on the kitchen table in 100 bundles of 50 twenties each. The total pile is a lot smaller than Don thought; it could fit in a shoebox. It is the price for his son.

He and Carrie sit and wait in the kitchen, while the police officers read the Monday paper in the den.

The call should come any minute.

Across town, at Quality Furniture, Billy and Skin follow their lunch routine on the shipping dock. They both sit on the edge of the concrete with their legs dangling back and forth.

"What a *total* fuck-up!" Billy says, loud enough to be heard inside.

Skin shushes him, but Billy has got to say it out loud: "How could that little son of a bitch have untied the knot, and where could he have walked off to? He might have slipped out right after we crashed. That would have given him about a six-hour head start. He could have made it to 74 in an hour if he could see. That's the only way out."

"Not likely," Skin replies under his breath. He feels very dark and gloomy, whereas Billy is just puzzled and pissed.

"You think somebody picked him up?" Billy turns to Skin. "Took him for a ride?"

"Shit, Billy, how would I know? All I know is that we're here, which is where we've got to be until this thing dies down, and there's no Lincoln in the president's space in the parking lot. Now, like you said earlier, let's just be normal, ok?"

"How much weed we have left?" Billy is looking for something to put this out of his mind.

The bell sounds and they push themselves upright and start in.

Then Billy grabs Skin by the elbow and jerks him back. "His blindfold was on, wasn't it?"

Skin just walks on, telling Billy to leave him alone and heading back into work.

————————

Don, Carrie, and Laney sit and wait for the phone to ring. It does, several times, but none of the calls are about Matthew. Each time, the nerves of all three of them crystalize and threaten to shatter.

Don paces in the kitchen. "What in God's name can be going on? I got the cash, and it's now 2:30. We're 30 minutes overdue, and there's no call. Is this just a game to them?"

Laney suggests that they probably are going to use a pay phone and maybe somebody else is using it.

"For 30 minutes? Now 35?"

"Mr. Harwood, I don't know. I really don't. It's not like there's a pattern of behavior here to go on. Each one of these situations is different."

"What if they don't call? What then?"

"Oh, they will. Trust me. How else are they going to make this worth their while? It's in their self-interest to call." Laney's voice is steady and assured.

Don collapses into a kitchen chair. The small suitcase full of bills sits next to him like an obedient dog, eager to go out for a walk.

At 3:00, the promised call still hasn't come, and a switch trips in Carrie's head, just like that, like a clicking snap of the fingers. She understands, with a mother's prescience, that the call will not come today. She fears it will never come. She stares straight at the oven but sees her angel boy with his golden, wavy hair backlit, like the sun forming a nimbus behind a floating cloud. Matthew is looking brightly at her with his blue eyes.

"Matthew!" she says aloud.

"Mommy . . . ." only she hears.

"Where are you?"

Don looks down to the kitchen floor and thinks not this again.

Laney looks puzzled.

Then Carrie sees the golden image of Matthew fade into black and white, and his countenance fades into the gray background.

She rises and walks over to a watercolor of a Bob White. It's one of the ones with an eye like a raindrop. She looks at the eye closely, and it looks back at her, into her. She sees the world upside down.

"He's dead," she announces solemnly, matter-of-factly, still staring at the bird's eye. "He's dead, and we are never going to see him or hold him again. My baby is *dead! Dead!*"

"I'm not supposed to tell you, but . . ." the bird replies before Don twists toward Carrie.

"Don't talk *nonsense*," he almost hisses. "It's gonna work out. It *has* to work out. It always does. You just need to rest."

"He's *dead*, and I might as well be, too."

———————

TUESDAY   When Billy and Skin pull into QF to punch in by 8:30, they notice that Don's car is still not there, but that there is a black Ford Fairlane sedan in his spot. From the license plate, they can tell it's a county vehicle.

"Shit and shinola," says Billy, while Skin's eye twitches. "Let's just keep our cool, bro."

At 10:00, Wally Deleau asks Skin to come with him. Skin gives a sideways glance at Billy and tries to breathe easy.

Wally says to Skin, "Look, I don't know what this is about either, so just go on in."

This is Skin's first visit to QF's offices since he was interviewed and hired. He is now standing at the same table he sat at for his interview, but this time he's across from Detective Laney, who holds Skin's QF employment file. The room is blue with smoke.

"Sit down, Mr. Johnson. I just have a few questions for you. First one is if you want one?" Laney extends the pack of Camels.

"No, sir. Don't smoke those things. What's this about?" Skin asks.

"Mr. Harwood's child is missing, so we're talking to every employee of Quality Furniture to see if we can get some leads. Do you know the child?"

"No, sir."

"How well do you know Mr. Harwood?"

"Not well. He's the boss. He hangs out in here while we're out at the shipping dock."

"Where were you Saturday night, say from 8 to midnight?"

"At Willie's. It's a bar on the west side. Me and Billy go there most weekend nights. Pool, pin-ball, cold beer. We were there from maybe seven until eleven. Then home."

"Who's Billy?"

"Oh. Billy Burns, he works with me out on the dock. I'm bunking with him now until I can get my own place.."

"Got any names at Willie's that could vouch you were there?"

"What's vouch?"

"Who could say you were there?"

"Willie's one; he's the owner, as you might guess. And the new girl, Christie. And some regulars too. What happened to the kid?"

"Well, that's what we're trying to find out. Thanks for your time. And can you ask Billy to come in?"

"Sure. I hope you find the boy."

Laney leans back.

"How'd you know it's a boy?"

"I... just guessed."

After a few minutes, Billy comes in for the same drill, and he gives basically the same answers, especially when it comes to the alibi. The only real difference is when Detective Laney asks him if he's got a record.

"Speeding, couple of times. Parking meter, that kind of stuff."

"Ok. Thanks for your time."

Pending confirmation from someone from Willie's, Laney scratches them off of his list of suspects. He reasons: why would they be at work if they had the boy and were going to trade him for cash?

BOOK

2

Between Time

With no further communication from the kidnappers, Laney convinces Don and Carrie to go all-out public. Within an hour of making calls, a *Citizen-Times* reporter and two TV crews arrive at the front door. Next day's headline will read: "Local Boy Kidnapped. Police Chase Leads," followed by the bizarre story of the ransom note, the calls, the deadline, and then total blackout silence, with no promising leads. A school picture of a half-smiling Matthew will accompany the article. The evening local news on ABC and CBS will be more sensational, with lines like, "the pajama-clad boy was apparently yanked out of his open bedroom window... no one in the neighborhood heard his screams... no word yet on whether he has been abused." The reporters will go on *ad nauseam* about all the things they do not know. Then for the next week, until a new story supersedes this one, they'll keep repeating, "the police still do not know..., and there is no information...."

Don also contacts the advertising firm that handles the QF account, and they quickly prepare a missing person flyer to be handed out and posted on telephone poles. It shows the same school picture of Matthew and gives a police number to call.

Laney tries to persuade Don and Carrie to offer a reward, though he does caution that it will bring out a lot of kooks and cranks and con-men. Ultimately, Don and Carrie agree to this as well. Soon the missing person flyers are replaced by the reward notice, carried in the papers and on TV and posted around Buncombe County on poles and two billboards: "REWARD. $25,000 for Information Leading to the Arrest and Conviction of Those Responsible for the Kidnapping of Matthew Harwood, Age 10, on October 7, 1972."

But no reliable information ever comes. Week in and week out, nothing ever comes.

There is little for Don and Carrie to do now but wait in the wilderness of their indefinite grief. They are two small boats tethered to the same limb while the river slowly slides by.

What comes are Carrie's parents. They were in France when it happened and find out about everything only when they return and hear Carrie's message on their answering machine. All Carrie says is, "Call me as soon as you get home, please." Her mother, Glenda, dials the number and repeats, "Matty! Oh, my God! Oh, no!" while Carrie's father, Richard, stands by asking, "What? What? What's going on?"

They drive up from Charleston in their Volvo as quickly as they can shower and repack. They arrive with large suitcases and move into the guest bedroom without consulting Don. By their actions, he can tell that they think they know better how to cook, clean, run errands, care, and comfort than their daughter, whom they still see as a child, and him, who they see as nothing more than an appendix to their daughter. Glenda says, "We're here as long as it takes," as she unpacks a Piggly Wiggly bag with its smiling pig face and clunks cans of beans and soup down onto the countertop. Her lavender perfume thickens the air and sickens Don. He notices that she has stopped dyeing her hair, and he stops himself before telling her that it looks like Spanish moss.

Richard small-talks from breakfast to bedtime like a fly buzzing in Don's ear. He spends an hour each morning with the local paper. "Hey, did you see they're gonna extend I-26 all the way to Johnson City? I don't see why the taxpayers have to pay for a road to somewhere nobody wants to go. What's there, anyway?" This prompts Don to leave for work, to look for Matthew, or just to get out. Carrie will mind the phone. He politely declines Richard's offer to ride shotgun on the long, slow drives looking for Matthew.

As Don drives away, he hears it over and over: "We're here as long as it takes." As long as it takes for what? For them to impress upon him once again that they never approved of him from the get-go, with his red-clay roots and all that comes with them—not to mention all that doesn't come with them—and now look how it's turned out? He has to roll down the window and stick his head out like a dog just to breathe.

Every time he leaves the house, he thinks about not going back. But he always returns. And each time, the house has shrunk by ten square feet, and he asks, "Anything?" The answer to which, from the three sunken faces, he already knows. "No. Nothing." To which he responds, as always, "Maybe tomorrow."

After two and a half weeks, Glenda and Richard finally come to realize that they have cared and comforted as much as they can, and that they might just be overstaying their welcome. Even Carrie is wearing thin, as it is easier for her to be alone with her sinking agony than to try to float above it with other people, even her own parents.

"Just call if you need us," Glenda says to her daughter, although Don is standing right there too. "You know we're just a few hours away. And I know you'll call immediately if …."

"Of course we will, and thank you so much," Don replies as he shuts the passenger door a little too quickly and starts waving goodbye.

After her parents drive off, it's just Don and Carrie orbiting each other. They stand a few feet apart, but it could be miles, invisible to each other, just chunks of matter near each other at the same time, each only abstractly aware of the other.

The unspoken rule is that laughter is forbidden in the house. Once, Don violates the rule and tries a joke that he overheard at QF. It falls to the linoleum floor in the kitchen like an egg that cracks and runs. All he can do is wipe up the joke with a paper towel and say, "I'm going out."

Their disavowal of intimacy is also unspoken. Neither talks of it. Neither makes a move toward it. They form parallel lines in bed, which they divide down the middle. It would be a sacrilege to move closer because it would dishonor Matthew's plight. Sometimes, they hold hands, but only briefly so. If they embrace, they do so sideways, shoulder to shoulder.

Despite her earlier outburst at the vision of Matthew being dead, Carrie sometimes talks to him about his homecoming and how she will hold him hard to the breast that nursed him and will never ever let go. How they'll go for chocolate shakes. Who they'll invite to a backyard party with an arch of colorful balloons. How just the three of them will go to the Isle of Palms or Pawley's Island for a week. She'll show Matthew the picture of him in the paper.

Lately, she can't make out what he's saying.

Otherwise, she says to herself it's funny—not meaning funny to laugh at—that, even in these most momentous of times, everything is still more or less the same as before: the skies, the clouds passing through on their way east, the pink sunrise that brightens and the orange sunset that darkens, the furniture that still needs reupholstering, the burn of grease that splatters from the bacon, the garbage to the curb on Thursdays, the black-and-white photo of Don, Matthew, and Paul and his dad squinting and smiling in the Smokies that she placed on the end table, the fuzzy teddy on his bed, the tinkling of the wind chimes hanging from the elm out back, the chill that follows the drizzle when wind whips up, the raindrops plunking down on her umbrella, the fireplace smoke-smell from two doors down, the slim hand of the clock on the mantle that ticks the seconds away and away and away. Everything appears ordinary, the same as before, except for one thing, the one dear thing that should have been her constant star.

Christmas comes and goes without a tree, without the three red stockings stitched with Matthew, Mommy, and Daddy. Carrie does not unpack the ornaments, candles, and other decorations. The fresh, minty, evergreen scent of a spruce does not permeate the house. They do not exchange presents. It is not a festive time. How could it be? The fly rod and reel that Wally mail-ordered for Matthew remains lifeless in a long, unopened box in the trunk of Don's Lincoln.

On New Year's Eve, after rejecting several invitations, Carrie stands in front of the kitchen sink finishing the dishes, with her back to Don, who leans against the door jamb to the den, eyeing the figure of his bride. Something moves inside him. He walks over and wraps his arms around her waist and says it right behind her left ear: "I love you, sweetie, come what may." She puts her soapy hands on his and turns her head toward his.

He continues, "Let's hope it's a Happy New Year."

But that hope in him summons up its nemesis in her. Carrie drops her head to her chest, and the moment passes by, crawls out the door, and is lost.

On January 15, 1973, Matthew's birthday, they invite Detective Laney over and show him the made-up bedroom, ready for the day Matthew would return. They ask him the old questions that he still cannot answer: Who did this? Where could Matthew be? What else could they do? What else could he do? Should they re-offer the reward, the flyers for which had long-since withered in the weather?

Meanwhile, the world turns, and other people and places populate the news, which Don and Carrie read and watch as a distraction from the obvious absence in their lives. The Dolphins beat the Redskins in the Super Bowl for a perfect season. Following the Paris Peace Accords, hollow-eyed American POWs are released by the Vietcong. The Senate Special Committee televises the Watergate hearings with a boyish John Dean testifying in front of the heavy jowls and eyebrows of North Carolina Senator Sam Ervin. Secretariat thunders through the thoroughbred racing record by winning the Kentucky Derby in 1:59.40. Jackson Browne

releases *For Everyman,* and Don listens to "I don't do that much talking…
these days I seem to think a lot… about the things that I forgot to do…
for you… and all the times I had the chance to…" before he gets up and
twists the plastic volume knob on the kitchen radio counterclockwise
until it snaps off. Spiro Agnew resigns and Nixon appoints Gerald Ford.
Henry Kissinger, whom Don and Carrie can hardly understand, starts
as Secretary of State. Nixon says he's not a crook and convinces no one.
Patty Hearst is kidnapped but joins her kidnappers in robbing a bank.
Billy Graham takes his evangelical crusade to South Africa then South
Korea. Hammerin' Hank Aaron smacks one out of the park and breaks
Babe Ruth's home run record to the joy of 55,775 fans at Atlanta-Fulton
County Stadium. O.J. Simpson rushes for 2,000 yards for the Buffalo Bills.
The reviewers say they like *The Sting* and *The Way We Were.* A TV reporter
in Sarasota shoots herself in the head on the air.

Carrie's old curse grows deeper in her despair, a despair that she
believes she exclusively owns. She starts to pick at Don. "You know it as
well as I do. If you had just fixed the damn screen!" At a complete loss of
what she could do that Don is not already doing, she continues, "Now if
you would please *do* something about this! Just *do* something Don, *do* it
now, to bring him back!"

Don hears her as if she were at the other end of a crackling long-dis-
tance line. He does not respond to defend himself or turn any accusations
back on her. Her words slowly fade away with smaller and smaller echoes.

Don does all that he can think of to do. He takes the reward posters
with him and drives all over Buncombe County. He approaches total
strangers and asks them if they have seen Matthew. He drives in and out
of Asheville, map in his lap, in parts of the city and countryside he did
not know existed. He asks, "Have you seen my boy? Here's his picture."
He drives and drives and looks and looks and is met every day with an
overwhelming, undermining nothing. He hears "sorry" a thousand times.
"Here, take this. Call the number if you see anything. Please." But no one

calls. And it's getting cold outside. And cold inside of his heart. And colder still wherever Matthew may be.

When Don takes his daily drives, Carrie secludes herself at home, wearing her pink terry cloth bathrobe day and night, waiting for a call or maybe for Matthew to simply walk in the kitchen door. Mommy? She hears around the corner. She looks, but there's no one there.

She refuses the sympathy of what feels to her like superficial want-to-be-her-best-friends. How could they possibly feel what she's feeling? How could they even remotely know her pain?

She sits. She folds and unfolds and refolds her hands. She folds and unfolds and refolds laundry. She folds and unfolds and refolds the last time she saw Matthew. She walks and rewalks the floors. She stares outside to the backyard but sees only a flat green blur. She has stopped painting because she cannot see the birds like she once did. At times she feels vacant inside, with her mind as barren as a desert. Other times, she churns with possessed thoughts that only a mother pining for her lost son can generate.

When she walks the floors, she passes her paintings. Sometimes she stops and converses, because those birds are real. She created them. They are her friends. One time, she stops too long. The blackbird's eye stares her down, looks into her as if he is ripping her wide open. She has been talking to him nice, asking about his day, but today he is in no mood for chit-chat. His eyelids are pulled back and his pupils are as narrow as a pencil point when he speaks: "You know you're the one who did it. It wasn't Don. It was you. You were the one who pushed Don into the river charity. You thought it would shine a light on you and make you the darling of the town. You pushed him. He did it for you. And if you hadn't gone to the ball and drank so much and danced so much and stayed so late, when your son was being stolen from his room, . . ."

"*Stop! Stop it!*" Carrie screams.

"It was *you!*"

She takes one last look into the bald, convex eye and this time sees herself upside down, heading down. It gets dark and cold quickly like nightswimming in the river.

Once a day, every day, Carrie asks Don when he is going to put the screen back on Matthew's window. Sometimes Carrie walks through the house calling out for Matthew like nothing has happened, like he's just in another room. Sometimes he answers her, I'm up here, or so she hears. But not always. And when there is no response, the house is as quiet as a morgue.

On one otherwise normal day—or as normal as it gets these days—Don comes home from work and sees that Carrie has put small band aids over the eyes of the birds in all of her watercolors. He walks all over downstairs calling "Carrie? Carrie?" with no answer. He goes upstairs and finds her in the bathroom. She sits on the closed toilet, face in hands.

"Carrie!"

She sits still, mute, deaf to his words. Blood is smeared all over her face. Don sees that the mirror on the wall is shattered head-high. Slivers reflecting light are scattered all over the floor. He should have seen it coming, with her as thin and fragile as an egg shell, but your mind just doesn't want to go some places. The mirror pieces crunch under his shoes as he steps to her.

"Carrie, sweetie, what have you done?"

Don pulls her hands apart and sees the slash on the top of her forehead. Her hair is matted to it.

"Jesus!"

As he rips tissues out of the box, cocks her head back, and dabs as gently as he can, she just says over and over: "it's over... it's over."

Don calls 9-1-1 for the second time in his life, and the ambulance takes her to Mission Hospital to get patched up, and then the doctor says that she has to go to the Fritzwater Institute to be evaluated. Don hopes against hope she hasn't slid back into it. They put those wrap-around restraining gloves on her, and Don follows the ambulance in his car. They start a mind-numbing drug they call chlorpromazine.

Don spends an hour with the psychiatrist and tells him what he didn't want anyone to know about the hell hole, how Carrie went down but then came back up.

After several days of evaluation, the psych doctor gets Don to sign the papers so Carrie can stay in a place where she can't hurt herself and hopefully can recover, like before. "We've got to do more tests, and I just can't see how it could be schizophrenia if she's been able to cope, or mask it, for so long," says the doctor.

"Schizophrenia?" Don cannot believe what he's hearing.

"Well, we just don't know at this point."

The doctor tries to reassure Don that, even if it is, it's not the end of the world.

The words easy for you to say rush down to Don's tongue but do not come out of his mouth.

The drug dehumanizes Carrie. She hardly speaks to anyone. Once found, now lost, she just looks vaguely ahead, or behind, no one can tell, with dark, dead, tranquilized, catatonic eyes.

In the kitchen, alone, totally alone, Don counts the days since October 7, 1972. Before coffee, as a daily ritual, he writes down how many days it has been since Matthew disappeared. *98* becomes *110*, then *133*, then *157*. On April 7, he writes *182* and under it *Six Months*, which he underscores and adds two exclamation points. Six months of the daily terror of not knowing. It would be far better to know. Without knowing, his imagination runs wildly and wretchedly through space and time day and night, and he sees Matthew here or there doing this or that, or Matthew suffering and calling out, or no Matthew at all. He can't shake the memory of the news of that six-year old boy from California who was kidnapped, imprisoned in a basement for three years, and raised as if he were the slave-child of the abductor. He managed to escape and run to the house of a neighbor, who called the police and returned the anemic and scarred nine-year old to his now-divorced parents. Yes, it would be far better to know, even if the knowledge were the most horrible thing he could imagine.

Counting helps Don try to define the undefinable, to interpose some degree of order into the chaos of his mind. That's why he still goes to work every morning. He rarely stays all day and, with Matthew and Carrie gone, has lost his passion for it. He pretty much lets Wally run the place. But the routine of the drive to work and the familiarity of his office and the good mornings from the workers provide an anchor that keeps his ship from drifting out, sloshing wave after sloshing wave, to the deep-fathomed sea.

200. Don writes it down. A human measuring time, as a way to understand and perhaps control it, as if he could. To divide into seconds, minutes, hours, days, weeks, months, years, decades, centuries—a fool's errand. Time is from everlasting to everlasting. It is seamless. There are no punctuation marks. One time, under God, indivisible. If someone asks you what time it is, you can't answer without time having already moved on. The monthly moon and the daily sun set on Don while they are rising on someone else. Everything, from whirling planets to rotating wheels, moves all around him, while he feels suspended above and beneath it all, in a place between time.

3

June 1974

In her second year as a summer camp counselor at Crossland south of Black Mountain, Maggie O'Shaunessy leads a group of ten girls hiking on the newly opened trail at the bottom of the west side of the rocky ridge that links Bat Cave to Chimney Rock. This is planned as a "Botany Adventure," to teach the campers about the native wildflowers: three-pedaled trillium, white-pink mountain laurel, violet Catawba rhododendron, delicate wood anemone, and so forth. She cautions the girls to be steady as they step on water-rounded boulders amid the flashing, rushing Broad River. They have already been trained to be on the lookout for copperheads and rattlesnakes. They also take note of the signs warning about possible rock slides.

Each girl carries a small backpack with her lunch and water. At Maggie's prompting, they sing a hymn that is their anthem at Wednesday evening chapel, with a crescendo for the final stanza:

> *Arise, your light is come!*
> *The mountains burst in song!*
> *Rise up like eagles on the wing;*
> *God's power will make us strong.*

The lyrics make them look up and feel good.

After hiking on the trail for less than an hour, they stop at a clearing about three miles in from where they parked the van and rest on boulders that the centuries have smoothed and that the rangers have arranged in a circle. Sunlight flickers through the waving leaves of the oak and poplar trees. Owing to an early morning shower, the blooming honeysuckle permeates the forest with the fresh and clean aroma of sweet tea with mint.

Maggie and the campers chew silently on peanut butter and jelly sandwiches and sip the metal-tasting water from their canteens. After the crunching of apples, Maggie brings out her pocket guide to the flora of the area, and the girls halfway listen to her. "What's this?" she asks while pointing to the picture of a rhododendron and covering the caption. Soon they pack up and, as instructed, leave no trace of having been there. The girls start to walk out in a line for the return hike.

"Wait." Maggie says. "Does anyone need to go? I do."

They all shake their heads, so Maggie pushes and pulls branches aside to get out of view. Even though they share the bathroom and the shower at the cabin, she was born modest. She makes her way about twenty feet from them, sets her pack on the ground, removes some tissue from it, checks to see that there is no poison oak in the immediate area, squats down, and begins to relieve herself.

Before she finishes, she looks straight ahead, eye-level, about ten feet away, and sees a pair of eyes, or rather a pair of dark eye sockets, staring right at her, almost right through her.

She screams.

Her startled heart beats like a tom-tom. She jumps up with her hand over her open mouth and steps back into something that scratches her in the thigh. She screams again and wheels around to see it's only a bush.

The girls are shaken when they hear her and think she's been snake-bit. Following the tallest one and her outstretched, waving walking stick, they all rush to the screams. They find her pointing and shrieking: "*It's a skull! It's a person's skull!*"

And there it is. A white skull, cracked at the top, with its jaw agape.

The girls join Maggie in screaming at the skull, which seems to scream back in a contest between the quick and the dead.

The immediate horror that the girls feel subsides when they realize that they are not in danger. Maggie, now more conscious of herself, pulls up her shorts and zips them. She takes the walking stick and gently prods the skull. It rolls toward her a few inches. They all shriek again.

Maggie pokes around the bush under which the skull had rested to see if a skeleton is nearby, but she doesn't see any other bones. She returns the stick to the tall girl, bends over, and, twisting her head, looks closely at the skull. After a minute of eye-balling it, she slowly reaches her right arm toward it, and then gently places her palm on the top of the head, as if she is baptizing it.

"*Ewww!*" the girls are equally repulsed and curious.

"Look," Maggie says as she picks the skull up and holds it under the sunlight, "look in here, a silver filling."

"The head's really small," says one of the girls, looking at Maggie, "smaller than yours."

"Is it a boy or a girl?" asks another girl.

"I have no idea," answers Maggie. "I guess they're about the same size. All I know is that we can't leave it here." She hands her stuff to one of the campers. They wrap the skull in the light windbreaker that Maggie had shed earlier in the day, slide it into Maggie's pack, and carry it to the van.

On the way out, Maggie feels like she is giving a piggy-back ride to a lost soul.

———————

A lost soul indeed. Matthew has weathered two winters and began his second summer lost and alone, quietly resting at the bottom of the cliff. The prods and knocks of Maggie's walking stick and now the jostling inside her pack loosen the memories long stored in his white skull.

His mother places three green tomatoes on the sunlit windowsill. Two, one larger than the other, are connected by the same vine. The third is separated and partially obscured by the smaller one.

"There!" his mother says with her hands on her hips. "You see? The Father, Son, and Holy Ghost!"

"They're tomatoes, Mommy."

"Ok, that's fine too. Whatever you see you draw. Better, whatever you feel you draw. Just don't make them flat. They need to bulge out from the paper. We need to see their depth."

Matthew stares at them. They stare back. Several minutes pass before he picks up his number 4 pencil and begins to shape the one in the foreground.

Maggie turns around to call out to a straggling camper, and her pack swings sideways and clunks into a small maple trunk, stirring another memory.

His father pulls into the driveway early and honks the horn with two short beeps, which he never does. Matthew walks out the kitchen door and sees the grin his father is trying to swallow.

"I wonder what got into my trunk today. Can you help me find out?" His father gives Matthew the keys. Inside is an open cardboard box bulging at the sides with the biggest pumpkin Matthew has ever seen.

"Cool!" Matthew tries to lift it out but can't budge it. So, together, father and son move the pumpkin to the front steps.

"Whew! Now, can you go get a Magic Marker and your good pocket knife?"

When Matthew returns, his father asks, "Happy or sad? Scary or nice?"

"Happy scary with an evil smile!"

By the time Carrie arrives in the cool dusk, pumpkin seeds and slimy innards are scattered all over the steps, and the hands of both father and son are sticky orange.

Matthew waits for the rebuke for making such a mess, but his mother simply says, "Beautiful! You have created a beautiful monster of a pumpkin!" She mimics the pumpkin as she bares her teeth and smiles at Don and Matthew. "Now, while you clean up this little mess you've made, I'll go find a candle."

After dinner, Matthew lights the candle and breathes life into the happy, scary pumpkin. He names it Spooky. All three sit down and watch the yellow light dance on the blue-stone steps. Don puts his arm around Carrie, and Matthew leans a sleepy head onto her lap.

Before he knows it, he is being carried by his father upstairs.

And then, in bed, he hears his mother start to sing:

> *There is a young cowboy, he lives on the range...*
> *And closing his eyes as the doggies retire,*
> *he sings out a song which is soft but it's clear,*
> *as if maybe someone would hear,*
> *goodnight you moonlight ladies, rockabye sweet baby James,*
> *deep greens and blues are the colors I choose,*
> *won't you let me go down in my dreams,*
> *and rockabye sweet baby James . . . .*

Another clunk as the van hits a pothole, and the skull in Maggie's pack is jolted.

Matthew feels relief at last when he uses the broken tree limb to scratch and pull the blindfold off. He holds his hands out straight in front of him to keep from bumping into another obstacle in the blur of the coal-dark night. He pats his right foot forward and puts his weight on it and then does the same with his left and takes another step and then another toward home. He fears the men may wake and come after him, so he quickens his pace. On the tenth step, the ground suddenly falls out under him. He frantically reaches for something but grabs only air. The wind howls past his ears as he whirls around and down and around and down until the crack! in his head. And then it is darker than any night, and so quiet and still, like when you bury yourself under all the covers until you can't breathe anymore.

The police dispatcher receives the call from the head of Crossland Camp, and soon Detective Laney is driving his Ford Fairlane towards Black Mountain. They summon Maggie to explain, and she is able to point to exactly where they made the discovery on a topographical map. Maggie says they looked but did not see any other remains close by. Laney has her write out a statement and she signs it. He then snaps several photos. Before he leaves to transport the skull to the station, Maggie asks how old it is and how long it had been there, to which Laney says that all those questions would be for the county's Medical Examiner, possibly even the state's forensics lab. Of course, Laney thinks he knows all the answers already.

He places the skull in the passenger seat and cushions it with that day's paper, the front page of which describes President Nixon returning from a trip to the Middle East only to face a possible impeachment vote by the Judiciary Committee.

Within an hour, Laney carries a manila folder and the skull into the Medical Examiner's lab.

The Medical Examiner holds the skull under a bright florescent light and rotates it. He focuses first on the same thing Maggie did: the silver filling. "We'll do the tests, but I can tell you right now that the DOD is between one and two years ago, and that the victim is a child somewhere between eight and twelve."

He then picks up the folder that Laney brought in and reads the label: "Matthew Harwood. Kidnapped 10/7/72. Unsolved." He says with a coroner's grin, "You're not trying to influence my objective analysis, are you?"

Laney responds, "Some things are just apparent and don't need a lot of figuring out."

The Examiner opens the folder and flips through the police report, the missing person and reward flyers, and the medical and dental records. He picks up a magnifying glass and holds the dental x-rays up to the light. "Ok," he says, "I'm not going to bet against you on this one. I'm going to x-ray the skull, but this is pretty obvious. This is where I'm glad I'm me and you're you, 'cause I don't have to make the call to the boy's parents."

"Yeah. One of the perks of my job."

After having crested as one of the most sensationalized and notorious unsolved mysteries in the state during the months after Matthew disappeared, the case has been cold for over a year, with no leads, no developments. There is nothing to report that has not already been reported. People have not forgotten, it's just that most of them have moved on to their regular lives and preoccupations. What else could they do but give and receive their daily bread?

Detective Laney has not spoken with the Harwoods since they invited him to their house on January 15, 1973 and told him it was Matthew's eleventh birthday. Now, in June 1974, Laney thinks that Matthew would have grown to about five feet tall. His face would be turning from a boy into a teenager. He would have just finished the sixth grade. Maybe he'd be on a Little League team.

Laney cannot bear the thought of calling the Harwoods out of the blue with the tragic news, but it's his job and he must tell them before news leaks out some other way. So, instead of calling, he drives to Sunset Parkway at 6:00 on this otherwise normal Wednesday evening. He sees their neighbors doing ordinary things like tending to their lawns, and he smells the distinctive, keen smell of city water that passes through a rubber hose before it sprays out in glimmering undulations across the grass. In the park-like median in the center of the loop, several kids toss a Frisbee, waiting for a call for dinner. The maple leaves turn and wave their white palms, the first sign that sweet summer rain is coming.

Laney walks up the front steps and knocks on the door. He has rehearsed what he will say, but nonetheless a single, cold bead of sweat runs down his spine before his belt catches it. There is no response, so he knocks again, louder this time. He hears the deadbolt slide free, and the door opens partway, with a noticeably aged Don Harwood holding the inner knob.

Laney looks at Don, and Don looks at Laney. Neither speaks. Don can tell from Laney's look why he's there.

"Come in," Don manages to say, and they walk wordlessly to the kitchen and sit down.

"Is Mrs. Harwood here?" asks Laney.

"You don't know? But then how would you?"

"Sorry. Know what?"

"She's been at the Fritzwater since last January. She couldn't deal with herself any longer over her despair about Matthew, and I couldn't care for her." Don feels he needs to add: "It's what the doctor said was required for her own protection."

Laney sighs. "I didn't hear. I'm so sorry."

"Well, it's not something I broadcast. So, go ahead and tell me what you have to tell me."

"Just on the other side of Bat Cave, at the bottom of a rocky ridge, a group of campers stumbled upon the remains—some of the remains— of your son. Actually, it was just a skull, but it's now been positively identified as Matthew's, from the dental records. I'm very sorry to have to tell you."

Don stands and looks out to the backyard. A squirrel sits up and holds his front legs together before he hops three times his height onto a tree trunk. Don knew this was coming someday. Despite hoping against hope, he knew, as a practical man, that there was little to no chance that he would see his son again. He had gone over in his mind countless times how he would react when it finally happened.

He feels the weight of the universe descend down on him.

Several silent minutes pass before he comes back to the table and sits next to Laney.

"I want to see it. I want to hold it in my hands."

"Sure. Of course. It's yours. My people are done with it. And you can give it—him—a decent burial. May help you find some peace at long last."

Don frowns. "Funny. I never thought about burying him. Every day I see his face. Every day I remember him, as he was when he was ten. You know—but no you don't because I've never told you—the last time I saw him I tousled his hair, which kinda annoyed him because he was getting to that age where he wanted his hair to be just so. Truth is, on that night, I was thinking more about myself than of him. Carrie and I were going to go out, have a good time riding high. Then we'd come back, he'd be here like all the times before, and life would go on its happy way, onward and upward. Before we left, I didn't even tell him I loved him."

Don's heavy head falls into his hands, and he melts down. His grief, sewn deep into the lining of his soul, suddenly surges up to his eyes and pours out. Laney puts a hand on Don's shoulder but can't think of anything to say that would be of any use.

Don stops and leans back. His face turns hard. "Who did it?" he demands of Laney.

"Believe me. I wish I knew. But we're not any closer than we were. No fingerprints here. No witnesses here or anywhere. Not a trace. We'll comb the ridge, but it's been a year and a half. Most likely your boy fell, or was pushed, but pushing doesn't seem to fit. Why would they do that if he was their ticket? Nobody could survive that fall. Straight down. He must have died instantly. One of my guys thinks there's a cave on the ridge, and it may have been the hole-up. We're going to look very carefully, of course, but so far nothing."

Don slaps the kitchen table flat and hard, and the salt and pepper shakers bounce off. Laney almost jumps out of his chair.

Don swears to himself that he will find and kill the son of a bitch if it's the last thing he does, but he knows better than to say it out loud. He paces and slaps his right fist into his left palm. He is strangely conscious of his movements and doesn't know how he is supposed to act.

Then he settles down and sits down. He asks Laney if he can follow him to the station.

"Sure you're ok?" Laney asks.

"I'm definitely *not* ok, but I want to go there."

And so they do, with Don following Laney in his car through the newly arrived drizzle, then following him through the door, then into the evidence room to a cardboard box. Laney opens the top, and Don peers in. He does not know what he expected. He sees a small skull resting on crumpled newspapers. It doesn't look like Matthew, but how could it? Matthew was flesh and blood.

Neither he nor Laney speak. From another room he hears the crackle of the police radio. Don reaches in and lifts the skull of his son out. He rubs his thumb over the crack at the top. He holds it up and looks at the teeth and the sole, silver filling. He turns it around and furrows his brow.

"That's the case number," Laney explains.

On the back of the white bone, someone had written neatly with a black, felt-tip pen: 1974-131.

Don turns the head so that they are face-to-face. He lifts it and looks into the dark eye sockets.

Then he kisses Matthew on the forehead, a father's lips gently touching the cool, flat, white bone behind which a boy's hopes and fears once swirled.

He returns his son to the box and closes the lid. It seems surreal to him, especially with the bluish florescent light. Living, breathing, golden-haired, blue-eyed Matthew Harwood is now 1974-131 in a cardboard box.

"Thank you," he says softly.

"You'll just need to sign the log before you go."

———

Back home, Don is confused about what to do. The box is an unfitting, undignified resting place. He places the skull on the kitchen table, and it stares at him. He walks it into the den and sets it on the mantle, where it looks like a trophy. No, that won't do. He picks it back up and roams from room to room. What is the proper, decent thing to do with the skull of your child? Maybe it should go in his bedroom. Don walks upstairs and props Matthew next to the pillow, and the skull still stares at him.

Don sits on the bed and says they have to talk.

"I'm sorry."

"It wasn't your fault," Matthew says.

"Your mother thinks so. She says it wouldn't have happened if I had fixed the screen."

"Where is she?"

"She went away for a while. She hasn't recovered from you being gone."

"Have you?"

"No. I never will, but your mother and I aren't exactly the same. I guess I'll have to tell her. Maybe we'll drive over together to see her in the morning."

"That would be nice."

At a little after midnight, Don awakes almost nose-to-nose with the skull. He utters a guttural sound and jumps back and sits up. The skull is sleeping, so Don turns out the light and goes to his bed, exhausted.

In the morning, he tells Matthew they are going for a short ride. He wraps two linen dinner napkins around the skull and nestles it inside his backpack, the one he took on the Mount Le Conte hike. Then he drives to the Fritzwater Institute.

A nurse is just leaving Carrie's room when Don walks up.

"How is she?" he asks.

"The same. She had an injection an hour ago and is pretty fazed now. You can go in, of course, but don't expect too much."

Carrie is on her back with her arms straight by her sides on top of the sheets. Her face looks better than Don remembers from previous visits, except for her eyes, which are wide open and stare at the ceiling. Don steps next to her and touches her hair.

"Hey," he says. "I'm here."

If she hears him, she either cannot or doesn't want to respond.

Don closes the door and pulls a chair beside the bed. He sets the backpack gently on the floor. What now? He does not have a precise plan. He could—maybe should—leave, and come back when she's more alert. He sits for fifteen minutes, looking at her, looking out the window, looking at his shoes, looking at the ceiling, looking at the two watercolors of hers that he had hung on the wall opposite her bed (band aids removed). The silence is interrupted by his memory of her refrain: "Don! *Do* something!" He would have, if he had known what to do. No one gave him a plan for this. What could he have done?

He sits there. Without willing it, he lifts the backpack onto his lap, unzips it, removes the linen napkins, and places Matthew's white skull on top of the fuzzy blanket that covers Carrie's stomach. He places it so that it is on its side, like a tender child seeking comfort and resting his head against his mother's hollow womb.

Don raises one of her hands and then the other so that they both cradle Matthew's head. He places his hands on top of hers, and they remain in this last family reunion until Don's lower back has a spasm. He looks at Carrie. Are her eyes wetter than when he first arrived? He can't be sure. Maybe he just hopes so. But he's done all he can do, given the circumstances.

"Sweetie, say good-bye to Matthew."

————

Don's next stop is the funeral home, where he and the director discuss what would be fitting and proper in these circumstances. Don almost chokes on the dead air. Then he says goodbye to his son and leaves him there. As he walks across the steaming asphalt of the vacant parking lot to his hot car, he feels as empty as his son's hollow skull.

When he returns home, he collects the *Citizen-Times* from the driveway. He unfolds the paper and stares at the front page. The headline almost shouts at him: "Skull Is From Boy Missing Since 1972. Reward Upped." The article is factual, not over the top, somewhat subdued for the press. It includes the statement Don gave last night before he and Laney went to the station: "As saddened as we are to finally have to give up hope of our son being found alive, we are all the more outraged at who could have committed such an inhuman act against a ten-year-old boy. Today we are increasing the reward to $50,000 for information leading to the conviction of our boy's murderer." The article also quotes Detective Laney saying that neither he nor his department will rest until they apprehend those responsible.

———

These days, Skin Johnson's right eye twitches even when he's sleeping, which is what he's trying to do before the rising summer sun breaks through the river mist and exposes his resting place under the bridge. His cardboard bed is damp, and he's chilled. His comforter is the heavy Army-Navy surplus coat they gave him at the last shelter, before he overstayed his welcome.

Through the fog of his dreams, he thinks he hears a dog bark. He raises his head and uncurls his frail body. Doing so, he dislodges the empty wine bottle that was his mistress the night before. It clink-clink-clinks down the concrete embankment, gaining speed, until it hits dirt and dies out.

The dog barks louder and nearer. Having been through this several times before, Skin sits up and raises his arms in surrender.

The black dog is thirty feet away at the end of a taut, leather leash. Picking up Skin's distinctive scent, the dog sits. The sheriff's deputy at the other end of the leash says, "You? Again? I've warned you twice already. You can't loiter here."

"Where else am I supposed to loiter?"

"Don't be a smartass. In the shelter. We've had this conversation before."

"They kicked me out."

"Look, buddy, that's not my problem. I've got to bring people like you in for trespassing, especially since I warned you twice. Come on. Get up."

"Do I get free bed and breakfast?"

"Smartass!"

———

At 10:00 the next morning, Skin sits in a metal folding chair at a metal folding table in the common room of the county detention center waiting for his court-appointed public defender, who is 30 minutes late. There's a newspaper in the trash can, so he retrieves it and slaps it open to the front page headline about the Harwood boy's skull being found under a rock cliff just outside of Bat Cave. He sees that there is now a $50,000 reward being offered for the murderer.

Skin leans back. "Jesus," he mutters. He shuts his eyes and puts his index fingers on his temples. He thought he had rid himself of it, but he hadn't. He can't. He is outside the cave, Billy's gone, the boy's asleep, and he touches his yellow hair in the autumn sunlight. As if he were his son. He remembers telling the boy it was going to be all right, but then it wasn't. If Billy had tied the damn leash on him, if he had stopped Matthew from wandering off, if.... And now it appears that no one had picked him up and taken him for a ride.

Skin shakes his head and reads the headline again. "Fuck a duck!" he says to the room of indifferent delinquents. "Just fuck a royal duck!"

"Excuse me?" Says a petite lady in a blue business suit behind him.

Skin jumps up. "Excuse me, ma'am. You snuck up on me."

She sees the paper and the headline on the table. She has already read it, as has everyone in town.

"It's tragic. It's un-Godly what happened to that boy. Can you imagine how terrified he must have been? And now, his poor parents .... But we only have a few minutes. We're in Room E. Let's go."

Susan Troxler is two years out of the University of Tennessee School of Law, where she was on the Moot Court team. She is back in her home town of Asheville to get as much in-the-trenches experience as she can before applying for a litigation spot at a private firm. She is paid by the county to represent vagrants, low-rent tenants, defaulters, and minor offenders, and typically her caseload overwhelms her ability to get to know her clients or do them any lasting good. She and the other public defenders refer to themselves as "wham-bam" lawyers, though they seldom get a "thank you, ma'am."

Behind closed doors in Room E, she asks Lawrence Johnson to explain how she can help him avoid the misdemeanor of trespassing on county property.

"Nobody calls me Lawrence. It's Skin. Skin Johnson. I've been called that so long I don't answer to Lawrence."

"Well, the judge is going to make you answer to Lawrence Johnson. That's how you're written up. So, tell me about why you were sleeping under the bridge."

Skin's face goes slack as he thinks, something he's tried to avoid for the past few years.

"I have to know something first. Because I'm not as dumb as I once was. What I've got to know, no bullshitting and no weaseling around with a lawyer's fancy words, is if this conversation is just between you and me. 'Cause you work for the county but you're supposed to represent me. And the county and me are at odds in this situation."

"Look, I've worked very hard to be a lawyer, and I hope to be one for a long time coming. If I violate the attorney-client privilege—which means that I have to keep what you tell me to myself—I'd be disbarred and lose everything for myself, not to mention the other women who are trying to break into this profession."

"Sorry. I didn't follow all of that. All I want to know is whether you swear that this discussion is just a secret between you and me."

"It is, Mr. Johnson."

Skin stands up and paces. Then he sits down and rubs his chin. He looks at Susan and starts to feel good about her. She may be his ticket. She looks and talks sharp enough. "You saw the article about the boy who was kidnapped—did you see the part about the reward?"

"Yes." Susan squinches her face up, not knowing where this is going, though she's used to her clients burning their precious time with her by going off-topic.

"I think I can get the $50,000, and I'll split it with you if you can help me."

Susan thinks Skin is as full of shit as the last guy she saw, but she's trying to be professional. "Tell me what are you talking about. Tell me how you need me to help you. If you have the right information, you go directly to the police and tell them."

"I can't do that."

"Why not?"

Skin hesitates. "I need the protection first, and I need my lawyer, you, to protect me."

"I'm sorry. You've lost me."

"You swear this is just between you me and you?"

"I already said it is, unless you're planning to commit a crime."

"I'm not. That's all out of my system."

Susan squinches her face again, leans forward, and folds her arms on top of the table. "Then I'm all ears."

Skin sizes her up and sees she's not all ears. In fact, she looks pretty good for a woman lawyer.

Susan uncaps her ballpoint and writes the date at the top of her note paper. "Well?"

"No notes."

Susan recaps her pen and her voice goes flat. "I don't have all day. I'm already late for the next guy. And I don't have time for bullshit."

"This isn't bullshit. I know who did it, who kidnapped that boy. I know the whole story. The only problem is...."

Skin clams up, and his forehead gets a little clammy.

Susan shuffles her papers and makes like she's leaving. "I told you I don't have time for games."

"The only problem is... I'm part of the story. I didn't kidnap him, or kill him, but I helped."

"Perhaps you didn't hear me. I don't have time for bullshit." She stands to leave.

"Sit, just sit down. I'm telling you as my lawyer. I know who did it, but I need protection."

Susan sits. "You mean protection from who did it?"

"No. What's it called if I get a deal with the D.A. that I can walk if I tell everything?"

"Immunity?"

"I want that, a deal so that I can walk. Then, when that's all official, I can tell you and everybody else."

"Listen. They're not going to give a deal to anybody, especially someone who is 'part of the story,' unless you give them something to go on. They will need credible evidence. Hard, specific, believable facts. Details of when, where, how. That sort of thing. They'll grill you to make sure you're not making this up. Because you're of no use to them unless your testimony can convict whoever did this."

Saying this, Susan thinks Skin is just messing with her. Over the last two years, she has been led down one too many rabbit holes, such that she looks at every new client with disbelief. And this guy, Skin, was brought up on trespassing and now he's talking immunity. Do they really think I'm naïve because I'm a woman?

Skin sits on this for a while. His mind searches back to that Saturday night, trying to think of something about that night that would prove he was there without giving too much away.

"Ok. Here's something, a little tidbit. Call it a teaser. The night the boy was taken, the babysitter had a guy over, and they were doing it on the sofa downstairs. Me and... me and this other person saw it clear as day. Made the other person's job a lot easier, because the girl was distracted."

Susan is speechless. Up to this point in her young career, she had defended against misdemeanor charges. This was not only a felony, but a sensationalized case that had already driven the media into a froth. And the man sitting across from her, her *client*, to whom she had just vowed secrecy, was saying he took part in a kidnapping that ended with the death of a ten-year old boy.

"You ok?" asks Skin.

"Yeah. Sure.... If you know all this, why didn't you come forward earlier? It's been over a year."

"I kept thinking the boy was alive. That he'd just walked away and been
picked up by someone and was alive. Maybe I was just fooling myself so I
wouldn't get all sucked up in a guilt trip. When I saw the paper out there,
it was like the gig was up, and I realized I was just kidding myself all along.
He was a nice boy. I liked him.... I tried to spring him but the other guy
stopped it, and then it was too late. He was gone. So I saw the paper out
there and something changed in me, like my insides did a flip. Like I had
blindfolded myself and someone just ripped it off. I even .... I'm blabbing
too much. I need a deal first. If I can walk, I'll talk. I know who did it and
where he's at."

Billy is at his uncle's place northeast of Weaverville, about 15 miles from Asheville. After Quality Furniture laid him and Skin off, Billy's uncle hired him to
help out with his small-time auto repair shop. Billy runs errands for parts and
basically does whatever his uncle tells him to do, which includes running
some moonshine at nights to trusted patrons and, most recently, running
some harder stuff that seems to be in favor with the local college crowd.
The uncle pays Billy cash, so there's no tax problems for either of them.

Billy sits on the front steps as his uncle walks up the paper from the
end of the gravel driveway and begins to open it. The front page blares out
the headline.

"Geez. Remember that story about the missing kid awhile back?" The
uncle asks. "They found his skull. And now there's a $50,000 reward to
find who done it."

A chill descends on Billy, from head to toe. He still sits, motionless, looking out over the cut grass, which appears to tingle in the summer breeze.

"You hear me?"

"Yeah. I hear you. That's too bad."

A reward, thinks Billy. A $50,000 reward! Where the hell is Skin?

Billy hasn't seen or talked to Skin in over a year. Skin wanted to stick with Billy and get the same deal working for the uncle, but Billy told him there wasn't enough work for the two of them. So Skin stayed in Asheville, where he could be more anonymous but also unemployed, broke, and homeless. Last time they accidentally bumped into each other, Skin was bumming from the sidewalk next to a gas station where Billy was filling up. The encounter was brief, and their deed was unspoken. It was past history. Nothing you could about it now. There wasn't anything Skin said or did that made Billy suspect that Skin begrudged him for moving on and leaving him behind. Or was there?

Skin did not begrudge him at first. But things can eat away at you when you're bumped out of rehab after rehab and shelter after shelter and have to find dry cardboard to sleep on before it turns damp with dew and then you're hauled in for the third time and people treat you worse than a mangy dog because that's what you look and smell like. More and more often, that's what you feel like, too.

―――――――――

The next day, Susan is bleary-eyed from having stayed up late in the public defender library researching topics she had already forgotten from her criminal law courses in Knoxville. Fortunately, it's not rocket science, and she relearns the protocol of what is necessary to secure immunity from prosecution in exchange for cooperation. In a case like this, it's a stretch for the D.A. to let anybody off scot-free, but they don't have anything at all without Skin. They can break a cold case with him and get a belt-notch conviction. They can get one or none.

Her boss is on vacation with his family so she calls the D.A.'s secretary to set up a meeting with just Detective Laney, the D.A., and herself. The secretary chuckles when she asks if the meeting can take place that day, saying, "you've got to stand in line, lady—how about July 10?"

"Tell them it's about the article in the paper yesterday, about the boy who was kidnapped."

"Can you hold for a minute?"

A few minutes pass before the secretary comes back on and says, "Will two this afternoon work?"

"Yep," says Susan, "but this has to be just the three of us, and no leaks to the press or anyone else. No grandstanding."

"I'll tell them."

_____

As Susan is led into an oak paneled conference room, the D.A. greets her with a politician's handshake, putting his left hand on top of their shaking hands, like they're old friends or she's one of his constituents. He introduces the rest of the assembly: Detective Laney, an Assistant D.A., and a uniformed sergeant.

"Please sit down," the D.A. says.

"Thank you," Susan says while continuing to stand, "but I made it clear that this meeting was just with you two." She points to the D.A. and Laney.

The D.A. responds with open palms, "We're all friends here."

Susan holds her ground: "It's either the three of us or there is no meeting."

She locks into the D.A.'s eyes, and he sees she's serious. "All right, gentlemen, we'll catch up later." They resentfully excuse themselves.

"Ok. You called this meeting. What do you have for us?" asks the D.A.

"I represent a client who knows the identity and whereabouts of the kidnapper and murderer of the Harwood boy."

"What's your client's name?"

"I am not authorized to tell you that at this point."

"Come on, counselor, you know that the identity of your client is not privileged information."

"It's a confidence that I am ethically bound to keep secret."

"Look," Detective Laney interjects, turning his head sideways to blow out blue smoke as he stubs out his cigarette in the ash tray. "The article in the paper just came out this morning, and already we've received over ten calls from phonies. How do we know that your guy has any valuable information? How do you know?"

"He gave me what he described as a 'teaser.' He said that when the boy was kidnapped, he and the perpetrator saw the Harwood's babysitter and her boyfriend 'doing it' on the sofa downstairs. Those are his words. That's all I have for now, but for what it's worth, I was also skeptical at first, but I now believe he's legit."

Laney stops breathing but keeps his poker face. He reaches for the pack of Camels.

"What else do you have?" The D.A., leaning back in his leather chair with his arms folded, is trying to act like he's not impressed.

"As I just said, I have nothing else at this point, and I won't have anything else unless my guy gets complete immunity. Then he'll talk. Then you'll go to the grand jury. Then you'll arrest and convict, with my guy telling the judge and jury everything you need for a life sentence, if not the death penalty. Then you can run for mayor. So, are you going to draw up the papers?"

"How do we know that your guy wasn't the mastermind?"

"When you see him, I think you'll agree that's highly unlikely."

Susan is on her way out of the conference room door when she turns and says, "I almost forgot. He wants the reward, too."

Susan exits the building into the heat of the July afternoon and puts her sunglasses on. Her initial giddiness about being involved in a big case and maybe getting her name in a newspaper article that her parents would see starts to give way to a sickly, sleazy feeling that she is trying to help a kidnapper and perhaps child-murderer walk free from a felony charge. But, she tells herself, a lawyer is supposed to take on unpopular causes and less-than-desirable clients; that's what Atticus Finch did. That's what lawyers do, they represent their clients zealously within the bounds of the law. So if immunity was within the bounds of the law, and that's what her client was entitled to, in the discretion of the D.A., so be it. After all, according to Skin, he and she would play a critical part in the process of capturing and convicting the really bad guy. And one is better than none.

———————

About an hour after Susan leaves the D.A.'s office, Detective Laney almost burns his hand opening the door to his oven-like, black Fairlane. He had already planned to attend the 4 p.m. grave-site service for Matthew, and now he has news for Don Harwood, a positive development on an otherwise mournful day. Nobody else knew about the babysitter but the Harwoods and him. This might be the real deal.

Laney drives slowly through Riverside Cemetery and sees cars parking bumper-to-bumper under the rows of lace bark elm trees that line each side of the drive. A flock of starlings bolts up from one of the trees, inks the sky with a figure-eight dance, and returns to the same tree. He parks, puts on his jacket, and clasps his hands in front of him communion-style as he walks up to the back of the solemn assembly. Don sees him and nods. Laney looks to see if Carrie is there. She's not.

A small, solid cherry-wood casket, custom-made under the personal supervision of Wally, rests next to the excavated earth. Laney, a hard-knocks kind of guy, has not anticipated how poignant, even eerie, it would seem to him that the regular child-size casket holds nothing but a skull. Instead, he tries to picture Matthew the way he looks on the flyers.

Dr. Porter is the first to speak. Predictably, he goes on about how Matthew had accepted Jesus Christ into his life when he was baptized, and how Matthew is in a much sweeter place now, walking in Heaven and talking with his Savior and Redeemer, who died to save his soul. At least he didn't say sinners, Laney thinks. Porter talks religion and reads from Corinthians: "O death, where is thy sting?" He has little to offer about Matthew as a person. At the end, he says that Mr. Harwood has a few words to say, and Don steps forward.

Don opens his mouth but can't get a word out. His throat is constricted, and his tongue has turned to sandpaper. He looks down to try to compose himself. Everyone there looks down as well, out of respect for him. Don swallows and looks back up. His face is red and quivering, but after a painfully long minute he sighs and gains control.

"The first thing I want to say is that, when I bought these plots several years ago, I envisioned that I would spend a long, full life with my family and at the end, when I passed on, my son Matthew, then a grown man, would be here saying a prayer for me. Now it's the other way around, and you can't imagine the grief of a father burying his only child."

Don looks up to the hills and takes a deep breath.

"We had so many months of agonizing about where he could be and what had happened to him. Now we finally know he's gone, and it's like a ton of bricks falling down on you. I want to get through this, but you'll have to bear with me, please.

"The next thing I want to say is what you already know. Carrie is not here with us in person, but her heart, her boundless heart, is here. I asked her doctors, and they said she wouldn't be able to stand it. She has been so fragile, and I couldn't let her break down beyond where she is now. I told her about the discovery, but she didn't seem to . . . ."

Don looks down again and counts to ten. Everyone else studies the grass or their shoes, until Don sighs and resumes.

"This small, beautiful casket contains all that is left of our beautiful boy. The fact that he died over a year ago does not take the sting out of it. Not in the least. My heart has been stung by bees from Hell and will be swollen for a long time to come."

He takes a brief, sideways glance at Dr. Porter, and everyone seems to understand that belief does not and never will numb the pain of the death of a child.

"Matthew was Carrie's prince of light. Whenever she would get down about this or that, his radiance would brighten her. She was so proud of him, especially his drawings and what a good reader he was. They shared something so very special. His sudden disappearance broke her heart, broke her spirit, broke her to pieces. It was like an essential part of her was stolen away into the night.

"He was my boy, too, and we shared a love that only a father and son can share. It was a love that did not have to be spoken, yet today I wish I had spoken it more often. Just watching a ballgame together, wrestling on the den floor, or planting tomatoes seemed enough at the time. I was planning on getting him fishing gear so we could stand together in a creek and I could watch him learn to cast and to catch a trout. But now that will never happen. Nor will I see him graduate from high school or college or find a girl and settle down and maybe get married and have a boy or a girl of his own. Those things will never happen, because he was taken away from us before we could say good-bye.

"So, here, I say it with all of my true heart and soul: Matthew, I love you, and your mother loves you. We'll love you forever and always remember you as our good and shining prince of light. Good-bye, son."

Don stands in silence, as do all of the mourners except two couples: Carrie's parents, and Paul's mother and father, who squeeze hands hard and fail to suppress their emotions from spilling out.

Then Don kneels beside the cherry casket, puts his hand on it, and bows his head. In his other hand is a piece of note paper that Paul's mother had given him yesterday. She copied from the Book of Numbers, and Don reads: "The Lord bless you and keep you ... The Lord lift up the light of his countenance upon you, and give you peace. Amen."

The gravediggers lower the casket.

Don, hollowed out, rises to embrace the dazed assembly: Carrie's parents, Paul and his parents, Wally, and other friends and neighbors.

He is the last to leave, or so he thinks. He sees Laney leaning against one of the elm trees flicking ashes onto the pavement. Don walks over and thanks him for coming.

Laney tosses his half cigarette down and grinds it with his sole. "You don't need to thank me. I would have come anyway, but as it happens,

I've got some information for you. It won't stop your pain. I don't think anything will, but it may help to know what happened."

Laney knows he's not exactly playing by the book in revealing information that has not been officially confirmed. But he thinks it fitting for Don to know. Especially on this day.

"A witness came forward. We haven't spoken to him yet, only to his lawyer. He says he was one of the two who kidnapped Matthew, and he's willing to talk, to give up the other guy, if the D.A. gives him a free ride."

"Jesus! You got one! Thank God!...But, what do you mean, a free ride?"

"He'd get off if he names the leader and testifies against him. This is all preliminary, but I wanted you to know."

"He'd get off? Just like that? You've got to be kidding."

"No, I'm not kidding. It's a cold case, and we don't have anything else. It's been almost two years."

Don knows how long. October 7, 1972 to June 20, 1974 is 621 days, to be exact.

"Do you think he's real?"

"My hunch is yes. He says he saw the babysitter with her friend in your den on that night. He wouldn't know that unless he was there."

"Well, you're not going to do it, right? I can't believe that anybody in their right mind would allow this guy, this *murderer*, to walk."

"Well, he's all we got, and we don't have him yet. If we work something out with him, we can nail the other guy. It's either one or none. And I'll take one over none any day."

Don's black-and-white memory of the night of the kidnapping now flares back in vivid color. He gets the same horrid feeling that he got when it sunk in that Matthew had been stolen, like his insides were thickening into concrete.

"Jesus," Don walks away rubbing his forehead. "This is way too much for one day."

Billy cruises the streets of Asheville looking for Skin. They need to talk, to make sure they're on the same page. Billy thinks surely Skin wouldn't do something so stupid as to implicate himself as a co-conspirator, or whatever they call it. Unless he's at rope's end. I can tell him we can work him into the business someway. $50,000! That's what Skin's share would have been, if they had pulled it off, and if Billy would have shared it and not changed his mind and decided to lickety-split out of town.

On College Street, Billy thinks he sees Skin, has to be him, who else looks like that, but he's walking toward the courthouse steps with a woman in a suit and heels. She holds a black brief case. Billy jams on the brakes and almost gets rear-ended. A horn sounds. Skin and the woman turn to look.

"Son of a bitch!" The AC is on and the windows are up so no one hears him.

The horn again. Billy tells himself: act normal, this could be something else, go home, act normal, just lay low. Skin and the woman move out of sight. Billy eases up on the brake and glides away, to lay low for a while and act normal.

BOOK

4

Breach Inlet

For Don, the funeral was way too much for one day, and the last two years have been way too much for one lifetime. Too much being constrained and compressed by Asheville, after worrying about Matthew, jumping whenever the phone rang only to be let down time and time again.

The trial of Billy Burns is months away, and Don needs to get away to somewhere completely different, to a place where you can see the sunrise and the sunset from the same spot. He has to get out of the mountains and to a place where you can smell the salt air and hear the waves falling all over themselves as they race to shore: the Low Country of South Carolina.

Except for several weekends visiting Carrie's parents in the confined swelter of downtown Charleston, Don has not returned to the beaches there since he and Carrie were in college and their respective fraternity and sorority houses had rented run-down clapboard houses over spring break. He remembers the late nights at the Sea Side pavilion with its funky soul bands and beer-infused, twirling shag dancing, and barefoot walks on the soft sand with the buttermilk moon rising out of the Atlantic Ocean. He was 21 and she was 20. They were just about to fall in love. Later, they would give each other rings and make promises they vowed never to breach.

And now here he is again, after a four-hour drive, and after so much of his life has been turned upside down and inside out, rolling down his windows to let the pungent marsh air blow in, cresting over the draw bridge to Sullivans Island, catching a glimpse of the shimmering sea. He turns left on Jasper and crosses Breach Inlet to the Isle of Palms. Before he checks in to his weekend apartment close to the pier, he stops at a red-dot store. He buys a cold six-pack of Miller High Life, which becomes a two-pack within a couple of hours.

At 10:00 p.m., after a dinner of fried local flounder, okra succotash, and coleslaw, he learns that the Sea Side is now called the Windjammer. For a ten dollar cover they offer a cover band and a free view over the railing out back of bikinied girls playing beach volleyball under the spotlights.

At 11:30 he feels full of beer and switches to gin and tonic. At midnight he says what the hell and slides off the barstool and stands at the periphery of the dance floor. The people shag no more. Instead, they dance apart, each to his or her own. Don is anonymous here. He starts to shift his weight from side to side. His arms rise with fists that roll around themselves like the moves the back-up singers did a decade ago. He feels more and more fluid, but to everyone else he looks like Pinocchio yanked on strings by a puppeteer with a sense of humor.

At 1:00 a.m. he is somehow dancing with the same woman for three songs straight until she says she needs some fresh air and they go out to the deck, where she says her name is Gloria, and asks his. Don tells her before thinking and puts his right hand over his left to conceal his wedding band. She looks out to the lace of the waves lit by the spotlights. She is younger than him and pretty in a rough way and looks really good in her red flowered dress, which the sea breeze plays with. Don asks her where she's from and she says West Ashley. He tells her he's from Lumberton, here on business. He asks her if she wants to take a walk.

At 6:00 a.m. he wakes to sight of red flowers disappearing and the sound of the door closing shut and the latch clicking neatly. He lifts his arm from over his head and sits halfway up. He squints to see that the covers on the other side of the bed are pulled back and the pillow is dented. *Jesus Christ!*

Don's head feels like a lead ball as he lays it back down. *Jesus Christ! What happened?*

He closes his eyes and tries to remember after the deck and the fresh air. They walked out to the beach. The moon was slender and the sky was sprinkled with stars. They must have walked here. They must have ... *Oh, God!*

Don bolts upright. "My wallet? Where my wallet?"

He lifts his crumpled khakis off the floor, and a palmetto bug zig-zags from under them to under the bed. His wallet is in the back pocket where it should be and everything seems to be in it and in its place.

Everything is in its place, except he's fallen in the breach on the wrong side of Breach Inlet and is disgusted with himself. He vows to forget his horrible mistake, which he stores in a small and dark compartment in the back of his brain.

He heads home by 9 a.m., two days earlier than he had planned.

———————

The dreary drive home in the July heat seems to take longer than the drive down. Don turns on the radio for a few songs but cuts it off after the commercials take over. He squirms in his seat and can't get comfortable. He turns the radio on again and tries for another station. It plays gospel songs. He cracks the window to give the AC a rest until he feels his back getting wet with the sweat of last night's beer and gin. He squeezes the back of his neck to lose some of the tension.

After Spartanburg, he begins the long ascent through South Carolina's Piedmont, foothills that will grow into North Carolina's mountains before he reaches Asheville.

He crosses the state line following a pickup pulling a trailer filled with someone's earthly possessions: a mattress, a dresser covered in a quilt, a full-length mirror, a metal table, a couple of chairs, and boxes. He is tired, his eyelids become heavy, and he doesn't bother to try to pass. What's the rush? To get home early and do what?

The pickup ahead suddenly swerves, followed in turn by the trailer. A chair dislodges and flies off the back. Don does not, cannot, react quickly enough, and the chair crashes into his front right. The pickup proceeds, oblivious. Don is angry at their failure to stop, adrenaline coursing through his system from the sudden jerk back to reality. He starts to speed up to catch them only to hear *flop-flop-flop-flop*. He has no option but to pull over.

By the time he does, his tire is completely flat.

Cars, trucks, and tractor-trailers whoosh by and splatter grit on him as he opens the trunk for the spare and the tools. He has to move the box aside to get to them.

He rolls the spare uphill on an asphalt shoulder that oozes tar. Then he hauls the jack and the tire iron up front. The sun beats down.

His hands are black from the spare. He takes the tire iron to take it out on the flat tire: he rears back and yells *son of a bitch* and slams the socket end into the rubber, which still has enough air to send the iron back straight into Don's shin. *Son of a bitch!!*

The job takes fifteen minutes, during which time Don's shirt gets completely soaked. He repacks the trunk and replaces the box. The box.

Don lifts it out and cradles it. It is the unopened box with the fly rod and other gear that was for Matthew and their trout fishing weekends. Up until now, Don has been afraid to touch it. Now, he opens the passenger door and lets it ride shotgun with him.

He changes plans, exits at Saluda, and heads for Snake Creek. He figures he has seven hours of daylight left.

After parking at a trailhead, Don opens the box to find basic gear. A six-foot long, three-weight rod; a reel; a floating line; a small plastic box of flies; fishing pliers; and, optimistically, a landing net. Within 30 minutes, he stands alone at the bank of the creek assembling the rod, affixing the

reel, and tying the end of the line to the eye of a Parachute Adams fly, carefully labeled in the box compartment.

Don removes his socks and shoes and rolls up his trousers to wade
into the chilly stream. He moves downstream within casting distance of a
dark-green pool that is preceded by a one-foot waterfall. He finds a warm,
semi-flat boulder to stand on.

His first attempts are jerky, and he tries to remember what Wally taught
him about being fluid and easy and patient. Once he gains his confidence,
he lands at the head of the pool and allows the fly and the line to drift. The
trout, if they are there, are not interested. Patience, they'll come to you,
he hears Wally say.

But nothing comes.

On the twelfth try, with an overarching back swing, he hooks the limb
of an overhanging Sycamore, and it takes a while to get as close to the limb
as he can and snip the line to free it. The fly will live on the limb, out of
danger, for a long time.

The compartment says the next fly is a Wooly Bugger, and Don ties it
on, regains the boulder, and begins to cast again to the dark pool. When
the afternoon sun breaks through a clearing in the trees and warms the
side of his face, he starts to think that catching a fish is not necessarily the
point of this. Maybe the point is the grace and peace of being alone in a
cool stream of pure mountain water rushing around and down with the
sun warming your face, and white Sycamores leaning over you standing
guard, and a lithe instrument in your hand like a divining rod.

He is alone, that much is true, and maybe the grace and peace will come
someday. At least this helps wash away some of last night's transgression.

He starts to hum *I come to the garden alone, while the dew is still on the
roses* ... and before the next line his line goes taut and pulls away. Don
flicks his wrist back and feels a stronger tug. One living thing connects
to another on the opposite ends of a taut fly line, and each can sense
something about the other. Trust thyself; have patience, Wally tells Don.

He gives some slack, and he and the fish take turns going back and forth about who is pulling whom.

Don alternately gives and takes and each time cranks the reel to shorten the line. He walks closer to the pool and sees his trophy resting with its red gills splaying. Their eyes meet, and the rainbow trout makes a gallant effort to escape. But the hook is set deep, and it is no use. Under the water, Don thinks it looks big, surely bigger than the one mounted in his office.

Don slowly drags his catch to the side, where the bank slopes into the creek. Soon the trout is out of water and looking uncertain with round fish eyes wide open. It flops until Don suppresses it with his left hand. He picks it up and holds it in front of his face. He can feel its pulsing heart.

"As beautiful as you would look mounted on my wall," Don announces to his catch, "I think I'm going to let you go, if you promise me one simple thing. Promise me you'll make more fish and pass on some of your beauty to them."

Don takes the pliers from his pocket and delicately extracts the hook. He lowers the trout back into the cool waters of Snake Creek and moves it side to side a bit to revive it. He opens his hand. The trout returns to its realm, after taking one look back.

5

November 1974

At 9:05 on Tuesday morning, everyone is seated in hushed anticipation in courtroom D of the Buncombe County Superior Court. Using the brass knocker, the Sheriff's Deputy strikes three times on the inside of the door beside the bench. He opens the door and stands at the threshold of the courtroom and booms out his formal, routine announcement: "Oye, oye, oye, all rise, this court is now in session, the Honorable Samuel Wright presiding."

The black-robed judge hovers in and plops down in his tall, cushioned chair. He surveys his domain and speaks: "Good morning, ladies and gentlemen. We're here to begin the trial in the case of the State of North Carolina versus William Burns. Are both sides ready to proceed?"

Both counsel rise. The D.A. and Luke Ramsey say, almost in harmony, "We are, your Honor." The D.A. neatly wears a three-piece, pin-stripe, dark-gray suit and a red tie. An American flag pin adorns his lapel. He stands with military posture and exudes the power of his office and the confidence gained from a string of recent victories in criminal cases much more difficult than this one should be.

Ramsey stands in contrast. Despite the fact that it is 45 degrees outside and on the brink of Thanksgiving, he is dressed in a beige summer suit with a blue and white striped bow tie. His shirt tail hangs visibly out from the back of his jacket. Ramsey wears glasses with a prescription of 0.0, in order to use them as a prop, to gesticulate or otherwise make the jury take notice. Under his strawberry hair, he has a ruddy complexion, and oftentimes his face heats up such that he fogs his glasses and has to stop, remove his handkerchief, and wipe them dry. It makes for a nice effect.

Ramsey has some criminal trial experience but is mainly known as a plaintiff's personal injury lawyer. He is no stranger to the courtroom and usually he tries—and wins—civil cases. A year ago, he took on Billy's uncle's case and got a respectable verdict against a woman who had rear-ended him and tore his knee up. That's why the uncle called and retained Ramsey, for a fixed fee of $10,000 up front, to represent Billy.

"All right, if there's nothing further, let's bring the jury in." Judge Wright instructs.

Within a few minutes, the jury is seated. They were chosen the day before after a series of *voir dire* questions that many of them resented, about their backgrounds, their jobs, their families, whether they could be fair, and so on. The chosen twelve consist of an accountant, three home-makers, a bank teller, a sanitary worker, a secretary, three unemployed people, and two retirees. Eleven white, one black. Five women, seven men. Several are anxious to hear the witnesses' testimony and the lawyers' arguments. The rest want this to be over as soon as possible and get back to their own lives.

After 30-minute opening statements, the first witness for the prosecution is Maggie O'Shaunessy, who testifies about finding the skull. She points on a map to the place under the rock cliff, and that place is then marked with an "X." Then Detective Laney is called and testifies that he took possession and personally transported the skull to the Medical Examiner. Laney also testifies that he interviewed Billy a few days after the kidnapping and that Billy denied any involvement and also lied about his prior criminal record for burglary. Otherwise, Laney has to admit that there were no fingerprints at the scene, no witnesses, and no clues until Lawrence Johnson came forward to identify the perpetrator. Laney is asked about what Mr. Johnson told him concerning Billy's involvement, but the judge sustains Ramsey's hearsay objection.

Judge Wright instructs the prosecution to call the next witness, and the D.A. calls Matthew's dentist, who is followed by the Medical Examiner. They both testify about the matching dental x-rays, taken when Matthew was ten and then post-mortem. The dentist adds that Matthew was an exceptionally nice boy. The Medical Examiner identifies the photos he took of the skull, and they are admitted into evidence without objection and passed around in the jury box under shaking heads and pursed lips.

One of the photos is enlarged and the D.A. places it on an easel in front of the jury. The Medical Examiner points to the crack in the top of the skull.

Q: Based on your examination of the skull did you deter-
              mine the cause of death?

A: Yes. Most likely it was trauma to the head, struck with
              some sort of hard object, which caused the brain to hem-
              orrhage, causing death within minutes after the blow.

Q: Where is the skull now?

A: We released it to the family, and I understand they
              buried it.

Q: Thank you. That's all I have for this witness.

The Court: Cross?

Mr. Ramsey: Yes, thank you, Your Honor. Doctor, you used a couple
              of words that I think the jury should listen to again. You
              said "most likely" it was a hard object that struck the
              head, did I hear you correctly?

A: Yes, sir.

Q: So, you're not certain it was a blow to the head?

A: Well, as you can appreciate, the skull had been out in

	the elements for, I believe I testified earlier, over a year, so I gave my professional opinion.
Q:	You mean your educated guess?
A:	In these circumstances, yes, given what I had to work with.
Q:	Just your guess?
A:	It was more than that. It is my professional opinion.
Q:	You will admit, however, that you are uncertain as to the cause of death?
A:	I am not 100% positive.
Q:	And this blow to the head—can I ask you about that? You understand that the skull was found at the bottom of a rock cliff that was 200-300 feet tall?
A:	Yes.
Q:	So the blow to the head could have been during the course of the fall, or on impact? He could have simply hit his head on a rock?
A:	That's possible, but I don't even know that he fell. I don't know where he was when he received the trauma.
Q:	You can't swear to this jury that a person inflicted this trauma to the head, as opposed to the boy simply falling off a cliff?
A:	I cannot.
Q:	Thank you. That's been very helpful. Nothing further.

Ramsey smiles at the jury. The D.A. frowns as the Medical Examiner passes between the counsel tables.

"The State calls Donald Harwood," announces the D.A.

Don wears a blue suit and wide, gray tie. He takes the oath, sits in the witness chair, and attempts a slight smile at the jury. He is interrupted by the D.A. asking him to state his full name and address.

In response to the D.A.'s questions, which he and Don have gone over twice, Don explains to the jury who he is and the events leading up to the kidnapping.

| The D.A.: | Let me direct your attention to the evening of Saturday, October 7, 1972. Can you describe to the jury what you remember? |
| A: | Carrie and I were going out to a charity function, and we were both focused on getting ready and leaving on time. The babysitter was there. It was pretty routine. Matthew and the sitter got along well. He and I had watched the baseball game together in the afternoon. He took a picture of us all dressed up. On the way out, I rubbed my hand on his head to ruffle his hair. It's a thing I did when he was going to school or we were going out. Just a playful thing. A loving thing, although I may have loved it more than he did. Anyway, we did that and left him in the care of the babysitter. We were going to be back by ten or so, and we said goodnight. The sitter said have a good time, and Matthew, trying to be funny, mimicked her voice but said have a good life. Those are the last words we heard him say, and that was the last time we saw him. |

Don speaks slowly and quietly, and when he is finished he looks drained, dry, and empty. The D.A. waits before he asks another question. The courtroom is so still you hear the old clock on the wall tick the seconds by.

Q:	And when you returned home?
A:	When we returned home, he was gone.
Q:	What did you observe?
A:	Two things. One immediate and one after the police got there. The first was a wooden ladder leaning against the wall under Matthew's bedroom window. And the other was a ransom note, which one of the officers found under the bed. Must have blown down there.

Q: Let me show you what we have marked as State's
                Exhibit 2. Can you identify this for the jury?

A: It's the ransom note. Somebody cut and pasted letters
                and numbers onto it.

Q: Can you read it to the jury?

The Court: Any objection?

Mr. Ramsey: No, Your Honor.

Don reads the note, which is then passed among the jurors while the
D.A. pauses.

Q: The note says you'll get a call the next day? Did you?

A: Yes. It was hard to hear because there was a lot of racket
                in the background. But the man on the other end was
                clear. I needed to get $100,000 in twenties by the next
                afternoon. He said he'd call back with instructions
                about how we'd exchange the money for Matthew.

Q: Did he say Matthew was still alive?

A: He didn't say. I asked, but he cut off the call pretty
                quickly.

Q: Did he call back?

A: No. We sat and waited. Didn't sleep. We sat and waited
                and there was not another call.

Q: Would you recognize the voice?

The D.A. turns and stares at Billy, who looks straight ahead.

Mr. Ramsey: Objection! The District Attorney is suggesting to the
                jury that the voice is that of my client, and there's no
                proof of that.

The Court: Sustained.

The Witness: I'd recognize it as *his* voice.

Mr. Ramsey: Your Honor!

The Court: Mr. Harwood, when I rule on an objection, you sit tight
                and wait for another question. You understand?

A: Yes, sir. But that's him. It has to be.

The Court: Mr. Harwood. You're out of order. Members of the
              jury, disregard that last remark from the witness. Mr.
              Harwood, wait for a question.

Don feels a sudden, searing pain in the back of his head, right above
the neck. Reflexively, he reaches back and presses a hot spot. He thinks
he's getting a brain tumor.

The D.A.:   Have you ever seen the defendant, William Burns,
              before?

A: Yes. He used to work for Quality Furniture. That's the
              company I own.

Q: Did you know him?

A: We met a couple of times, but we worked in different
              parts of the building.

Q: Did he know you had a son?

A: I'd bring Matthew out there, but I can't swear that *that*
              man was aware of his presence.

Q: Did the kidnappers ever call you again?

A: No.

Q: How did you learn of Matthew's death?

A: Detective Laney came by unannounced. I was at home.
              He didn't call, but I knew he or someone would knock
              on my door someday. I had tried to steel myself for it.

Q: Was Mrs. Harwood there too?

A: No. I had to have her committed to the Fritzwater Insti-
              tute, indefinitely. She and Matthew were so close, and
              she was unable to handle his disappearance. She hardly
              talks anymore because of the drugs they make her take.

Q: And how has all of this affected you, Mr. Harwood?

Mr. Ramsey: Objection. Relevance.

The Court: Sustained.

The Witness: Well, I . . . .

The Court: Mr. Harwood. What is it about sitting tight that you don't understand? I know this is difficult for you, but we all have to follow the rules. Anything further?

The D.A.:   No, Your Honor.

The Court: Any cross-examination?

Mr. Ramsey: No questions, Your Honor.

By their facial expressions and the way they shift in their seats, the jurors appear surprised and disappointed they won't see Ramsey cross Harwood. But Ramsey figures that nothing that Don Harwood said hurt his client. Besides, you don't want to attack the innocent father of the innocent victim.

In the hallway outside of courtroom D, Susan Troxler sits next to Skin on a worn wooden bench. Like on the night before he and Billy got out of the car, Skin taps his fingers on his thigh at ten beats per second. He and Susan have talked all they need to, and so they sit without speaking, watching lawyers walk by with an appearance of purpose.

Skin sees the black of night for a moment and then sees Matthew standing and walking away. Skin opens his lips as if to say stop. But nothing comes out. The boy disappears.

"A deal's a deal, right?" he asks Susan.

"What do you mean?"

"I mean, I got the immunity thing, and they can't go back on it now, can they?"

"Not if you walk into that courtroom and tell it to the jury just like you told the D.A. and me. We went over this."

Skin leans back. Still looking straight ahead, he says, "I need a toke."

"Well, as your lawyer, I advise you that would be a very bad idea given where we are."

Then, out of nowhere, Skin says, "Since you're my lawyer, I'll tell you a secret. I did it. I let the boy go. Billy was asleep. He didn't do nothing."

Susan jerks her head 90 degrees to look at Skin, who doesn't meet her eyes. "What! You lied to me?" Her face turns hot.

"I told you what you needed to hear."

Susan stands to face her client. "Listen to me, you ...."

Before she can finish, the Deputy swings open the courtroom door and booms out: "Lawrence Johnson!"

Skin stands. "Here." And then to Susan: "Thought you'd want to know."

"Follow me," instructs the Deputy.

Skin does so, all the way to the witness box. Susan, still in shock and wondering what she should do, takes a seat in the back row.

As required by North Carolina law, prior to Skin's testimony, Judge Wright informs the jury that the testimony they are about to hear is under a grant of immunity from prosecution, and that he will give the jury guidance on this before they deliberate on a verdict.

Skin swears to tell the truth and averts his eyes from Billy, whose presence he can feel enveloping him like his conscience personified. Skin has a hard time ignoring Billy in the courtroom, even though that is what the D.A. told him to do. The D.A. advised him just to look at the lawyers when they were asking questions from behind the podium, then look at the jury when answering, and then it would be all over and he could leave this mess behind and move on with his life.

On direct examination, Skin pretty much tells it like it is, as the D.A. leads him chronologically through the events of October 1972. He does not deny his participation, but he does emphasize, as he had practiced with the D.A., that it was Billy who hatched the idea. At the D.A.'s request, Skin identifies Billy by pointing to him. That is the only time their eyes meet. Billy's eyes are stone cold. Skin's are darting. Skin testifies that it was Billy who planned everything out, who thought of the alibi, who snatched Matthew from his bedroom, who decided on the hole-up, who made the ransom call, who mistreated Matthew, and who let Matthew walk off from the cave into the dark, blindfolded, to his death.

Susan Troxler can't take anymore, especially Skin's last point. She stands from her seat three rows back in the gallery before the D.A. moves on to his next question. "Your honor," she states boldly.

Every head in the courtroom swivels to look at her.

"Your honor, may I approach the bench?"

"What the...?" the D.A. stops when he sees it's Susan, and he is not pleased she's interrupting his case.

"The witness is my...." Susan cannot get it out before the *crack* of the gavel.

"*Order!*" Judge Wright barks. "I will not tolerate disruptions! Any more outburst like that and I'll have the Deputies remove you. Do you understand me?"

Susan sits down. She must. What else can I do? She thinks. I tried.

The D.A. turns to the bench. "Your honor, may I proceed?"

"Proceed."

Skin sits up straight and hopes no one saw that his mouth had been hanging wide-open for the last minute. Was Susan trying to tell him something?

"Mr. Johnson, can you show the jury on this map where the cave is?" Skin points, and the D.A. writes "cave" directly above Maggie's "X." Skin says he was Billy's accomplice and was mostly stoned or drunk throughout the episode. He regrets that he fell under Billy's sway. He says he is very sorry and that he never intended to hurt the boy.

Susan's mind swirls as Skin continues to testifies. Has she just witnessed perjury by her client?

The D.A. turns toward Ramsey, extends his right arm back and then sweeps it forward, as if ushering him in, and says, "Your witness."

Ramsey takes his time gathering his notes and moving behind the podium. He hopes that his delay will increase the suspense and the attention of the jury. It does. Especially since the first questions on cross-examination go straight to whether the jury should believe Skin.

Q: If this jury convicts Billy Burns, you stand to receive the $50,000 reward money offered by Mr. Harwood?

A:	I sure hope so. I signed up for it.
Q:	And if this jury acquits Mr. Burns, you get no money?
A:	I guess not.
Q:	So..., your testimony is motivated by your desire to get the reward money?

Skin looks to the D.A. with wide-open eyes, looking for help.

Mr. Ramsey:	Your Honor, can you please instruct the witness not to look to the District Attorney for any assistance in answering my questions?
The Court:	I saw that too. Mr. Johnson, your testimony has to be yours alone. No one can telegraph answers to you. Do you understand?
The Witness:	Yes, sir. What was the question?
Mr. Ramsey:	Your testimony before this jury against my client is motivated by your desire to get the reward money?
A:	Well, to be honest, it's not... I mean I know it's out there if all of this works out... but I'm telling the truth.
Q:	How much do you make now?
A:	Zero. I'm unemployed now.
Q:	And $50,000 would be a dream come true for you, wouldn't it?
A:	Well, sure, it would be for anybody.
Q:	Just to be clear, you want Mr. Burns to be convicted so that you can claim the $50,000 reward?
A:	How am I supposed to answer that?
Q:	I think you just did. Now... let's move to a different topic. You remember that a few days after the kidnapping, you were interviewed by Detective Laney?
A:	Vaguely. It wasn't a big deal.
Q:	By your own testimony here, you had just participated in a kidnapping, and a detective is asking you

questions about whether you have any information. That's no big deal?

Skin's eye twitches and he doesn't respond.

Q: You lied to Detective Laney, didn't you?

A: Yes, but I'm telling the truth here.

Q: And until you saw the reward in the paper after the boy's remains were found, you concealed your part in the kidnapping?

A: I guess that's right. What would you have done?

Q: You didn't come forward with your account of events, where you say you were just following Mr. Burns like a lamb, until you got a deal from the D.A. granting you immunity from prosecution?

A: Of course, I needed protection.

Q: If you were subject to prosecution at this point, meaning you did not have immunity, and you stood to be convicted, you'd still be lying about the kidnapping?

A: Why not?

Q: Just one more thing, Mr. Johnson. You said you were drunk or stoned or both back in October 1972. So that period in your life was kinda foggy, wasn't it?

A: What do you mean?

Q: Your memory of events back then is not perfect, is it?

A: No.

Q: So it's possible that you don't remember things exactly as they happened?

A: Anything's possible.

Q: That's all I have for this witness.

The D.A. has no follow-up questions on re-direct because he does not want to open the door to re-cross. So he says, "Your Honor, the State rests."

Susan follows Skin out into the hallway.

"How'd I do?" he asks her.

"How did you do? You lied under oath! You could go to jail for that!"

"But nobody knows but you, and you're my lawyer. So, when can I swing by for the reward?"

Susan's blood boils like never before. "You worthless son of a bitch. *If* there is a reward, I'll make sure that you don't see a penny of it."

"Whoa, lady! Back off. We're in this together."

Before Susan can respond, with what she's unsure, Skin turns his back and walks off, down the hallway, down the steps, gone.

After a recess, the jury is hungry to hear what the defense will be, especially how Mr. Burns will try to explain himself.

Ramsey calls William T.S. Boggs, who explains that he owns and operates Willie's, a bar and pool hall on the west side. Mr. Boggs swears to the best of his recollection that every Saturday night in 1972 Billy Burns and Skin Johnson were at Willie's until at least midnight and that, as a team, they often won the nine-ball tournament and pocketed up to $100 in cash.

On cross, the D.A. holds up a calendar and asks Mr. Boggs how many Saturdays there were in 1972. Willie doesn't know exactly. So the D.A. makes a big show of counting. "Well, would it surprise you if there were 53 Saturdays in 1972?"

Willie replies, "No, that wouldn't surprise me."

The D.A. presses his point: "So, if there were 53 Saturdays in 1972, you can't remember for sure if Mr. Burns was there on Saturday, October 7, 1972, can you?"

Willie looks at the jurors with an open face. They can't tell if he's confused or caught.

"Can you, Mr. Boggs?" the D.A. will not relent.

"Well, let's see." Willie reaches into his shirt pocket and pulls out a small spiral note pad. He starts to flip through it.

"What are you looking at, Mr. Boggs?"

"I keep a note pad for every year. This one was for 1972. I write down things of significance to me and my business. What day did you say?"

"October 7."

"Ok. Let me get my glasses on. October 7. Here it is. I wrote this down: 11 p.m. Billy was out of line with a girl. Almost a fight. Told him to leave."

The D.A. tries to look like nothing of consequence was said. "Thank you, Mr. Boggs. That's all I have." He says with a smile so as not to appear he just got knifed in the side.

As Mr. Boggs steps down, Judge Wright instructs the defense to call its next witness. Ramsey rises, runs his fingers through his hair, removes his glasses, wipes them clean, puts them back on, looks up at the wall clock, and announces, "The defense rests, Your Honor."

The jury murmurs with surprise.

"Ok. So be it. Ladies and Gentlemen of the jury, we'll take a short break and then proceed to closing arguments. I remind you not to discuss the case with anyone until I have given you the jury charges and you begin your deliberations."

In his closing, the D.A., practiced in the art of confidence, begins with the heart-strings stuff of a ten-year old boy not only forcibly snatched out of sleep in his bedroom, but snatched out of life itself. The D.A. holds up side-by-side the school photo of Matthew and the photo of the skull. "Here once was youth and health and the promise of a wonderful life ahead, and here is the tragic, fractured skull of a dead boy. That was all that was left for his loving parents to bury. And who made the difference between life and death? *That* man: the Defendant William Burns. The evidence is unrebutted, and thus undisputed, that he robbed this boy of his life by a pre-meditated kidnapping for ransom, stealing a human being to trade for a suitcase full of twenty dollar bills.

"We did not bring this case lightly, and you should do your civic duty as jurors to take it as seriously as the most precious thing you value. Listen to the Judge's instructions, go to the jury room, and find that the State has met its burden of proof on the two counts of kidnapping and murder. Feel good about coming back in here to announce your verdict of guilty on all counts. That is the only way, *you* are the only way, for Matthew Harwood and his family to receive the justice they deserve. On behalf of the State of North Carolina, I thank you, and I trust you will do your solemn duty."

Now it's Ramsey's turn. He stands and walks over to the two photos, which he removes from the easels and leans against the jury box, out of view. In contrast to the bouncy style of the D.A., he is slow and ponderous, modulating his tone and volume. At times he pauses to let a point sink in. Some of the jurors lean forward to make sure they hear every word.

"I don't represent the government. I'm not a part of the bureaucracy or the politics. I don't run for public office. But I do represent real people, people like Billy Burns, people who have been falsely accused of crimes. And it's my job at this point in the proceedings to help you reach a verdict—the word means to declare the truth—a verdict that acquits Billy. What is at stake here is the liberty of a fellow citizen. You are the only people in the State who can keep him from going to prison for a crime he did not commit.

"Let me say here at the outset that Billy and I recognize the tragedy that has befallen the Harwood family. Our hearts go out to them. No family should have to face the loss of a child. You know that, and I'm sure you feel deeply saddened by the loss of Matthew.

"We certainly don't dispute that he lost his life. How he did so is a mystery, and even the Medical Examiner is unsure about how Matthew received a blow to the head. He could have simply stepped on a slippery mountain trail and fallen off a cliff. No one knows for sure. There's no proof somebody hit him.

"Now let's get to some basic protections under our law for a citizen who has been accused of a crime. These protections are for all of us, and you must honor them, as the Court will later charge you. First, the D.A.

got the grand jury to indict Billy. But the Judge will tell you that an indictment is not evidence of guilt. Second, Billy is presumed innocent. He walked into this courtroom as presumed innocent as you and me. Third, it's the D.A.'s job to prove to you that Billy is guilty beyond a reasonable doubt. When you think about the testimony and the evidence—and there are no exhibits except for the map, the note, and the photo of the skull, so we're really just talking about the testimony—each and every one of you must determine for yourself whether that testimony *fully satisfies or entirely convinces* you of the defendant's guilt. That's how Judge Wright will define proof beyond a reasonable doubt. He'll tell you it's the D.A.'s burden to prove guilt beyond a reasonable doubt. It's not Billy's burden to prove his innocence. So, are you, each of you, *entirely convinced* of guilt based on the witnesses' testimony?

"We might as well be honest: the only testimony here that you need to think about is that of Mr. Johnson. You'll have to ask yourself: Is he believable? The Judge will help you out in deciding that he was not. He will tell you to use your common sense in being the sole judges of the facts, including whether to believe Mr. Johnson. You should consider Mr. Johnson's demeanor, his ability to recall, whether he has any interest in the outcome of the case, and whether his testimony conflicts with the rest of the believable testimony we've received.

"So, I see some of you are taking notes. Please note these five points, because either separately or taken together, they tell you loudly and clearly that Mr. Johnson is not worthy of belief, and if he's not worthy of belief, you must acquit Billy.

"One, and most obviously, Mr. Johnson wants Billy to be convicted because he'll get a $50,000 reward. Ask yourself if that gold mine might skew his testimony, even compel him to lie.

"Two, and the Judge will speak to this, because Mr. Johnson made a deal with the dev... I'm sorry, with the D.A., you should examine his testimony with great care and caution. Rather than come in here and truthfully tell you what happened out of his good conscience, he made a deal to save himself. And you remember he said his testimony would be different if he didn't get the immunity from the D.A.

"Three, you saw him on cross-examination. His eye twitched just like a liar's. He would look to the D.A. to bail him out.

"Four, his memory is all shot by the dope and booze he was doing. He admitted as much.

"Five, his testimony directly conflicts with that of Mr. Boggs, the owner of Willie's, who said that both Mr. Johnson and Billy were at the pool hall on Saturday nights up until at least midnight, including October 7, the night in question. You heard Mr. Harwood testify that the boy was noticed missing at about 11:00 p.m. Mr. Boggs does not have a dog in this fight; he had no reason to lie.

"The State's whole case depends on your believing Mr. Johnson. There is no other proof offered that would link Billy to what's at issue here. Ask yourself: are you *entirely convinced* that Mr. Johnson told the truth? If you are not, you must acquit Billy Burns.

"I noticed that some of you seemed surprised that we rested the defense after calling Mr. Boggs. Some of you may have been surprised that Billy did not testify. From our standpoint, there was no need to call Billy to the stand because the D.A. simply had not proven his case. There was no need to belabor these proceedings and waste yours and the Court's time. In any event, don't take it from me. Take it from Judge Wright, who will tell you that North Carolina law requires you to *completely ignore* the fact that the defendant chose not to testify. The law gives the defendant, just like you and me, the privilege not to testify and assures that this creates no presumption against the defendant. The judge will instruct you that the silence of the defendant may not influence your decision in any way.

"One final point. You heard the D.A. say that Matthew and the Harwood family deserve justice. Well, we agree. But justice is a two-way street. *Justice... is not convicting... an innocent man.* Billy deserves justice, too.

That justice comes from your hearts and minds, from you as the collective conscience of this county and this state. That justice is a declaration of truth—your verdict that the D.A. has not *entirely convinced* you, and thus you should let this innocent man go free. All you have to do, and it's what you *must* do in this case, is check the little box next to 'Not Guilty.' From the bottom of my heart, thank you."

Judge Wright reads the jury instructions. He looks up after every one to make sure the jurors are paying attention. When he's done, he sends them to the jury room and tells counsel they can leave but to be on a ten-minute call.

Two hours of deliberations pass. Then, through the Deputy Sheriff, the jury foreman sends a note to the judge, who calls counsel back in and up to the bench. "They want me to re-read two charges: the one on burden of proof and reasonable doubt, and the one on the defendant's decision not to testify. I'm going to call them back in and read those charges. Any objection?"

"No, Your Honor," the D.A. and Ramsey say in unison.

The minutes crawl by in the courtroom as the jury deliberates behind closed doors. Not willing to risk being absent, the D.A., Ramsey, Don Harwood, Detective Laney, Susan Troxler, Billy's uncle, two reporters, and a half-dozen courthouse junkies wait. They can hear some animated discussion in the jury room, but all the words run together, and it is impossible to make them into sentences.

Minutes turn into hours, and finally Judge Wright says he's going to send the jurors home for the night, to return at 9:00 in the morning. He admonishes them not to speak to anyone about the case, or to watch TV or read any news articles.

Day two of the deliberations is totally uneventful until 12:26 p.m., when the foreman pushes a buzzer that causes the hearts of everyone in the courtroom to flip over.

One by one, the jurors file into the box and sit down.

The judge asks if they have reached a verdict.

The foreman stands and says, "No, Your Honor. We haven't. And we can't. We're deadlocked. We've tried, but we can't seem to come together."

Everyone in the courtroom except the jury slumps in their seats.

"Get me the Allen charge," Judge Wright instructs his clerk. Within a minute, the jury is told sternly and crisply that it is their duty to reach a verdict, that another trial would be costly, that each juror should hold to his or her honest belief, but that they should reconsider whether to accept their fellow jurors' views, and, in the end, if the evidence in the case fails to establish guilt beyond a reasonable doubt, the defendant should have their unanimous verdict of not guilty. Then the judge tells them to retire once again and continue their deliberations until they reach a verdict. He says he is prepared to stay late, even though it's Friday.

At 3:10 p.m., the jury buzzer once again electrifies everyone in the courtroom and lifts them out of their seats. As before, the jury files in and sits down and the judge asks if they have reached a verdict.

This time, the foreman stands, holding a few sheets of paper, and says, "Yes, Your Honor, we have."

"Hand it to the clerk."

The clerk reviews the verdict form to see if it is complete and signed by the foreman. Her eyebrows rise involuntarily as she scans the document. Then she tightens her lips and gives the verdict back to the foreman.

"You may publish your verdict," the judge says.

"I'm sorry. What?" the foreman asks.

"Read it out loud," the judge says dryly.

"On Count One, Second Degree Murder, we, the jury, find the defendant, William Burns, not guilty."

"Shit!" Mumbles the D.A., barely audibly.

The gallery murmurs, which causes the judge to strike his gavel down and order, *"Order!"*

Now it's Billy's turn for his eyebrows to rise. He sits up in his seat, expectant, but also knowing that a conviction on the other count could still send him to prison for life.

The foreman frowns at the D.A., then proceeds. "On Count Two, First Degree Kidnapping for Ransom, we, the jury, find the defendant, William Burns, not guilty."

Billy holds both arms straight up like he's signaling a touchdown. Ramsey turns to face him, and their awkward embrace knocks Ramsey's glasses to the defense table.

"*What?!*" Don Harwood instinctively jumps to his feet and screams. "*What?!*" His face is blood red and he starts to move down the aisle before Detective Laney grabs his arm and pulls him back. Ramsey stands as a blocking back in front of Billy.

"*Order!*" The judge demands again. He slams his gavel down: *Crack! Crack! Crack!* He raises his voice: "*Sit down!*" Then, as things quiet down, he swivels to the jury box. "Ladies and Gentlemen of the jury, the Court thanks you for your service. You are excused and may go home and about your other business. The Deputy will guide you out."

Several reporters scramble out to meet the evening paper deadline.

Susan Troxler sits in a state of total disillusionment.

"*Cowards!!*" Don hisses at the jury, who look back at him in the sharp light of reality after their detached deliberations. Don points at Billy, who is trying to disappear behind Ramsey. If it weren't for the decorum of the courtroom, the cracks from the gavel, and Don's innately measured demeanor, he would scream, "*I'll hunt you down you little son of a bitch!*" His contorted face pretty much conveys that message anyway. A Deputy intervenes and leads Don slowly back-peddling out of the courtroom.

Susan moves toward him and says, "I'm sorry, Mr. Harwood."

But Don's head is about to explode and he cannot hear.

The Deputy escorts him out to the parking lot, "That's a tough pill to swallow, sir, but you have to go on home, there's nothing left to do here."

Don sits in his Lincoln and wraps his arms around the steering wheel.

It seems the wheel is the only thing he has left to hold on to. The back of his head pounds, like when he was in the witness chair. He rubs his forehead on the top of the wheel, then slides back in the seat. He sees a reporter approaching, sits up, turns the ignition, and glides out with as much dignity as he can muster.

6

Evening

Don sits alone at the kitchen table watching the refrigerator The evening edition of the *Citizen-Times* lies scattered on the floor. After Don read the headline he tossed the paper like a Frisbee to the corner of the room. The headline blasts the news: "Shocking Verdict in Kidnap Case." Under it is the picture of a satisfied Billy Burns and a grinning Luke Ramsey, with the caption: "Defense lawyer says, 'The State simply did not prove its case.'" The article reports that the D.A. said that the jury had spoken, but declined to comment further. The continuation on A-3 once again trots out the picture of the once-happy Matthew that they used on the reward poster. Don reads an op-ed criticizing the D.A. for bungling what should have been an open-and-shut case, calling for change at the next election.

The phone rings several times, but he does not move to answer it. At least the reporters are respectful enough not to show up at his front door wanting an inane comment. He's sick and tired of that. He does not know what to do. He had hoped that he would be able to visit Carrie and tell her that justice has been served at last, even though it probably wouldn't really reach her.

Before he knows it, he is sitting on Matthew's bed. He has kept the room as a shrine to his son, who is lost to him in all things but in memory.

Don surveys the collection on top of the dresser, the sketchbook, the closet of clothes, the made-up bed, the teddy bear, and the window, now finally screened and closed. The back of Don's head pulses painfully when he thinks of Billy Burns celebrating with his clever lawyer and whatever scum he would count as friends or relatives.

His grief rises from inside him and begins to engulf him and overcome him. Then it turns quickly to hot-blood anger. *This is not enough!* Don whispers to himself, not knowing in the slightest what enough would be. He stands, rubs his neck, and starts for his bathroom to splash cool water on his face.

Before he takes a step, he hears two hard knocks on the front door. "God damn them to Hell!" He goes down the steps to tell them just that.

Without looking to see who it is, he unlocks the door and flings it open ready to yell *leave me alone!* only to see Detective Laney, who is holding a brown paper bag. He extends it to Don and says, "I thought you'd need this, and maybe some company."

With Don standing puzzled, Laney pulls a quart of Johnnie Walker Black out of the bag.

Don sighs and says, "Come in. You're about the only person that I'd take as company at this point."

Taking the last sip of his first glass of neat Scotch, Don realizes that the pounding in the back of his head has diffused into a slight and welcome buzz. He and Laney don't talk too much about the trial, as there's no use Monday-morning it. Laney steers the conversation toward college football, particularly the match-up tomorrow between Tennessee and Ole Miss. As the closest powerhouse, UT has many fans in Asheville, and Laney is one of them. He bemoans how the team just cannot keep up with Alabama, which is on its way to another SEC championship.

Don tries to get engaged in the discussion, but his mind is elsewhere. As Laney discusses the difficulties of the Vols, Don asks, "How do you get over something like this?"

Laney thinks for a while. "I thought I'd never say this, but maybe it's time for Coach Battle to look for another job. I mean, the team'd be lucky to get seven wins this year."

"No," says Don, "Not that. I thought with the guy getting convicted and heading to jail for good, I could move on. But now I can't. He's out there right now having a big party with my boy's blood on his hands. How is that how it's supposed to be? You tell me, how is that anywhere close to being right?"

Laney pours two more, and they sit there, each staring at his own glass. They could be in separate worlds, and, with their different backgrounds and minds and memories, to some extent they are. But they are still two men sitting at a kitchen table drinking Scotch from the same bottle to try to heal their fresh wounds.

After a bit, Laney takes his pack of Camels out of the side pocket of his jacket. "Do you mind?"

"No. Go ahead." Don stares longingly at the pack. "I gave those up twelve years ago, when Carrie was pregnant. Just went cold turkey and never looked back. But maybe now I'll have just one."

"Sure," Laney replies, and he lights one for Don, who takes a short drag and then puckers his mouth and slowly blows the smoke out as a whisper floating through the silent room.

"How do you get over something like this?" Laney repeats Don's earlier question. "I'm not sure there's a one-size-fits-all answer. Everybody's got to find their own way. I did, once, and it worked for a while."

"You did what?"

Laney tells Don about the drunk driver who smashed his pick-up truck into his wife's car, killing both of them, him instantly and her after fighting for her life in the hospital for two days. She was on her way back from Ingles with eggs and bacon for breakfast the next morning, and Laney's last words to her were to see if they have any salt-rising bread. When the police first arrived, her engine was running and the radio was on and the groceries had been hurled out on the street, salt-rising bread included. She had been hurled out, too, as this was before seat belts were required by law. She was all messed up and unconscious until the end.

He says he wished the guy had lived so that he could suffer, either because of his injuries or at Laney's hands. He lashed out at everything, since the guy he wanted to take it out on was gone. Not a day went by when he didn't imagine what he would have done to him: horrible, excruciating, torturous things, with him looking into Laney's eyes and knowing who it was that was slowly killing him.

He says it took him a long time to get through it, and he's really not all the way through it even 15 years later. The church stuff didn't work, he would never be able to simply forgive, even if God was happy to. It was way more complicated than that. In time, he backed off from it and put it in the distance, not because of the bullshit about the passage of time healing wounds, but because he read an article in *Popular Science* that started him thinking in ways he had never dreamed of. It was about how we are all just atoms stuck together for a finite period of time. The atoms were doing something else before they became us and they'll go off and do something else again after we're gone. So, when you think of it with that perspective, that we're just a collection of atoms, you can detach from the feelings that would otherwise make you puke day in and day out. Maybe you can lose some of the sense of responsibility for what you do and don't do.

"But your whole job is holding people accountable for doing bad things. How do you reconcile that?" Don asks through the haze of smoke.

"Oh, I do my job, and I'm pretty good at it. It keeps me from going too bonkers."

"So, with Matthew, you're saying you really don't care because in your mind he was just a bunch of atoms?"

"No. That's why I'm here. After all these years of seeing guys who done it get off and still just moving on to the next case, I don't think I can let this one go. I've always played it by the book, but, for this one, the book be damned. When, down the road, I look back and see what I've achieved and what I'm proud of, I want to feel good about this."

Laney, usually straight and blunt, eases into what he came to say.

"You ok to let it be?" he asks Don.

"Let it be?"

"Yeah. Just move on. Let time pass to heal the wound."

"I don't know what else to do. This all happened today."

"Well, I'm six months from retirement and a pension. So I'm just saying I'm ready to talk when you are, if you ever are, about how to bring some mountain justice to Billy Burns, to even the score. Things won't be right in the universe, at least in my universe, until that happens. I know where he's at and what he's up to in Weaverville."

Don has not eaten since breakfast, and words and thoughts and feelings are sloshing around in his Scotched brain. He doesn't know if this is just whiskey talk from Laney, or if he's just having trouble understanding. "I'm not sure I'm following all of what you said. It's just been a long and brutal day so far."

"I fully understand. As I said, whenever you're ready to talk."

"I'm sorry. I didn't thank you for the Johnnie Walker. And I didn't say how sorry I am about your wife."

"Sleep well, Mr. Harwood. You have my number."

Don walks him to the door and thanks him again. He shuts the door, locks it, and leans back against it, as bewildered as he has ever been. His mind is swimming with the liquor and with what Laney said. He's not ready to adopt the we're-just-a-bunch-of-atoms approach, although it rings a faint bell about a college course on Roman philosophers talking about the nature of things. How can we be just a bunch of atoms? What about the mind, the heart, and the soul?

It's too much for now. He goes back to the kitchen for a bowl of Grape Nuts, which he sees as just a bunch of atoms, and decides that he needs help from someone who knows what they are doing. Otherwise, he may end up sharing a room with his wife.

———

As Don heads upstairs to a bed that is too wide in a house that is too big, Billy Burns buys a third round of Pabst Blue Ribbons for everyone at Willie's. He does his touchdown dance for the third time, to the jukebox playing *Band on the Run* and *Bennie and the Jets*. After winning the nine-ball tournament, he takes the $100 cash prize and gives it to Willie, as a little thank you. He tries his hand at Anna, the waitress who is new from out of town, and she mistakes him for a local hero and takes him home later to a bed that is too narrow.

Meanwhile, Skin, holding his thumb and forefinger a quarter inch apart, tells the other two trolls under the bridge that he was *this* close to getting a $50,000 reward. He recounts how he handled the questions from the D.A., just like he had practiced, but then Billy's lawyer threw him some unexpected punches that weren't fair because he hadn't thought to rehearse the answers. Skin picks up on how the trolls may be thinking not so kindly that he's a snitch and maybe in with the cops. They stop talking with him, and he shuts up and then curls up on the cardboard. He worries that Billy is looking for him. That would not be a pleasant reunion.

By dawn, he's on the right-of-way on I-40 West with his thumb out and waving a crude sign that says, "Nashville." It won't be Florida, but it won't be here. I'll be out of Billy's reach. Maybe I can get a job washing dishes. Surely they must have some good weed there; that music stuff doesn't come out of nowhere.

Don is not the church going type. Never has been except for when he was a kid and for a little while after college, when he thought it might help his business. In Asheville, it does not look good if someone asks where you go to church and you say nowhere. It's better to say First Baptist and then go through all of the do-you-know-so-and-so, which could lead to more business. To be truthful, he probably would not have gone as much as he did—both before and after Matthew was lost—if it weren't for Carrie's insistence. After she was lost, mentally, he stopped attending. Business didn't seem important anymore.

But now he is lost and does not know how to find himself. What is he supposed to do? What in God's name is he supposed to do, with everyone and everything now lost: first Matthew, then Carrie, then justice itself, and now him too.

Don calls Doctor Porter of First Baptist, who directs him to an associate pastor trained in counseling. They meet at a small office at the church, and Don is impressed by how the young associate, John Bartlett, is so fresh and open and easy to talk to. Don lays it all out as truthfully as he can. There's no reason to hold anything back. He even says that he may not be able to come to terms with the situation unless he somehow makes Billy Burns pay for getting off with impunity after causing such a horrific, life-destroying set of events. John is relatively new to the church and thus was not there when Matthew was alive, but he says he has followed the news of the trial and knows the story.

"What do you envision doing to Billy Burns?"

For several days, Don has been rolling over in his head what Laney had said over the Scotch—about torturing the guy who killed Laney's wife, and about evening things out with Billy Burns. He rolls these thoughts over again before answering.

"I can't stop picturing strangling him with him looking right at me."

"And then what would you do?"

"I haven't got that far yet."

"Well, let's say you did that, strangled him. Wouldn't that lower you to the same level as him? Wouldn't you become like him?"

"It's different. He had no cause. I do. I'm avenging the kidnapping and murder of my only son. Doesn't the Bible talk about an eye for an eye and a tooth for a tooth?"

"It does, in the Old Testament, when retribution was a common theme. But in the New Testament, when Jesus brings his message of grace and forgiveness, it says something quite different. In fact, in the Book of Matthew, fitting for this discussion in many ways, it says to turn the other cheek and to forgive. Matthew 6:14-15. I can read it to you, but it basically says that unless you forgive those who sin against you, God will not forgive you of your sins. Let me try to put it this way: forgiveness is the path to *you* being at peace with yourself and with your God. Isn't that what you are looking for, at least to be at peace with yourself? Because you have to live with yourself and be at peace before you can come to terms with the situation, as you say. Otherwise, you'll be in turmoil—frankly you'll be in Holy Hell—for the rest of your life. So, forgiving is something you'd do for *yourself*, not for Mr. Burns. Wouldn't Matthew want you to do that? Wouldn't he want his father to be at peace?"

"That sounds nice, but I have no earthly idea how to even start that process, much less accept it."

"Remember that we are all children of God, but we all have dark spots inside of us. They're not all the same, and some people have more than others. You have them. I have them. And Burns has them. Whether we were born with them or grew them over time doesn't really matter. Some of the dark spots are dormant, but others can liquefy into bitter, black bile that will plague you and cause you to do things that you will later regret. With the light of God, you can put these dark spots to rest, you can forgive yourself for having them, and you can forgive Burns for having them as well. If all of that works, you find the peace that *you* deserve."

Don leaves the office unpersuaded. When he settles into his car, however, he realizes that the pounding pain in the back of his head has subsided. Maybe I should try it, he says to himself. It won't cost me anything.

Billy and Anna take to each other. For the first time in a long time, Billy falls headfirst in love. They see each other several times a week, usually followed by him sleeping over if it's not a delivery night. His hard head and heart begin to soften, and his acidic guilt— which he will never admit to himself or anyone else—lessens its corrosion of his insides. He actually sees a brighter future, a way out of the rut of his dangerous life of driving booze and drugs in the dark. He figures he'll need to work through the spring, until the college kids get out and go home, to save up enough to be able to figure out something else to do.

On Wednesday night, Anna gets off early and they meet up at their rendezvous bar, one that is quieter than Willie's. Billy orders the usual, a beer for himself and a Chardonnay for her, but before the word leaves his mouth she says, "Not tonight. Just a water for now." Billy screws his head around and asks, "You sick?"

"No. I'm fine."

"So, what's up with you? Not partying with me tonight?"

She looks at him straight on and looks a little scared, which she is. Her heart races. She manages a smile that she had tried on earlier in the day, and then she proceeds with the words she had rehearsed.

"Billy," she says. "Billy, it's a little early to tell for sure, but I think I'm pregnant. Pregnant with our baby."

Billy looks back at her straight on. It appears she's not joking. He can't think of what to say. They look at each other until her head drops and she looks at her lap and her folded hands.

Billy's mind starts to spin like a merry-go-round. Pregnant?

"Well, of all the things you could have said."

Her eyes get wet. She wipes them with the paper napkin.

Billy just sits there not knowing what to do or say. Then, flatly, "I thought you were on the....?"

Anna puts her hands to her face and swivels in the bar seat away from Billy. She begins to sob.

Billy begins to thaw. He reaches out and puts his right arm around her and squeezes her shoulder, causing her to swivel back slightly towards him. Her face is red and puffy and still hanging down.

Billy lifts her chin.

"Hell's bells, Anna, if you are, and we are, then… well, that's the best thing you could have said."

Right there at the bar, with a neon Miller Lite sign shining on them, they embrace.

"I love you, Anna."

"I love you, too, Billy." She pauses. "Can you imagine it? Our baby, crawling, learning to walk and talk? Before we know it, she'll be ten!"

"Or he'll be ten."

Later, after a talk about not telling anyone just yet, he walks her to her car and opens the door for her and says he'll follow her home.

He shuts her door, gently but firmly, and takes the first step in what will be his attempt to walk from his world of dark to her world of light.

"Wow" is all he can say to himself as he settles behind his wheel and cranks the engine. "Wow."

As he follows her home on the winding roads, turning left and then right and then left again, a box in his trunk falls over with a *thud*. Billy sits up straight, grips the wheel, and remembers. He starts to feel real sick in the stomach.

———

Ten days later, at their third session, John realizes he's not getting through the hard shell of Don Harwood. So he tries a different tactic.

"Can I tell you this story? I think it might help you understand what I'm trying to get across."

"Seems like you've already told me all of the stories from the New Testament."

"This isn't from the Bible. I think you're kinda Bibled-out. It's part of my story."

"Sure. Why not?" Don says while John closes the Bible and pushes it aside.

"I was senior in college, majoring in ancient history and writing my thesis paper on the Minoan civilization. I convinced my faculty advisor that I should spend the fall semester in Crete. What better place? I'd studied it and seen photos but I wanted to feel it—the blue sky, the pink rocks, the silvery olive groves. I wanted to walk the same dusty ground as did King Minos and breathe the same air that filled his lungs."

"You're getting a little poetic on me here." Don has never been poetic.

"Just listen."

Don leans back and folds his arms cross his chest to keep a barrier between himself and John's story.

John is animated as he tells of the joy landing on Crete and then a week later feeling the bottom drop out when he gets a letter from his girlfriend, who wrote she was breaking up with him and was seeing John's roommate. Don tries to pay attention but the time and the place and the people that John describes are so remote that the story doesn't gain traction in Don's mind. He intermittently hears about how John was furious, revengeful, and plotting. Dons hears bits and pieces of hiking some gorge, jumping off a cliff into the cold sea, and being rescued.

As John finishes his story, he gazes out the window.

He turns to Don, whose arms are still folded across his chest, just under his resting chin.

Now it is Don's turn to look out the window. He asks John, "Did you ever reconcile with her?"

"I forgave her. And I moved on as a better person. That's the point of the story."

"So did you get married to someone else and have a child who was kidnapped and *murdered*?"

Don gets up to leave. He feels strange and bad about not being politely sympathetic. He's not sure what's inside of him. "Sorry. Maybe next time."

For another month, Don almost forces himself to continue regular sessions with John. Gradually, Don feels that he is beginning to rid himself of his craving for revenge. Not that he is necessarily becoming religious; it is more like he is trying to maintain himself as a civilized human and not revert to some animal self.

Slowly, a weight seems to lift off of him, and he returns to the Rotary luncheons and tries to chat it up like before it all happened. He spends more time at the QF and is actually interested and productive. His future seems lighter, and he thinks of a variety of ways to reengage with life. He visits Carrie and tries, however unsuccessfully, to help her remember who she is and who he is and who their son was. He re-connects with three men in a golfing foursome at the country club. He and Wally take the afternoon off and fish for trout. He starts to walk in a new world, and, at just 38, he figures he has a lot more steps ahead of him. Maybe he will take up jogging, which people are starting to do in his neighborhood.

Then a simple act of kindness turns his world dark again. A late afternoon knock on the front door. It's Matthew's friend Paul and his mother.

"Hey, Don," she says, "Sorry I didn't call but I didn't want you to say no. We brought you a homemade dinner. I hope you like it."

Paul extends the double grocery bag, and Don takes it. "Well, thank you very much. I'm sure I will. Do you want to come in?"

They say no, because Paul has homework and needs to get ahead before the camping trip this weekend.

Don can't help staring at Paul, who looks down. "You've sure shot up since I last saw you."

"Yes, sir," is all that Paul says. His voice is deeper than Don remembers.

"How's your dad?" Don asks Paul.

"Oh, he's fine."

"Ok, well, we should be going," his mother says. "Let us know if you need anything."

"Thanks. Tell your dad I said hello."

They turn and walk down the sidewalk. Don closes the door and turns to the kitchen.

He sets the bag down on the table and sits in front of it. He smells it and knows what it is before opening the bag: pot roast, gravy, potatoes, and squash. He opens it and sees that, yes, it is the same thing they ate for their last supper with Matthew.

He pushes it away.

He rests his forehead on the table top and closes his eyes. The room begins to swirl around him. He was fine until this. He was getting over it. And now the dark sequence of events seeps back into his head and spins. The tousled hair. The brief goodbye that was not supposed to be forever. The dancing and drinking. The empty bed. The ladder. The police. The note. The call that came and then the call that never came. The flyers. Carrie. The skull. The trial. The look on Billy's face. The look on Billy's face. The look on Billy's face. The look on Billy's face.

He can't rid himself of that God-awful look.

He stands and is drawn like a magnet to Mr. Johnnie Walker.

He drinks the fire to burn out images.

It doesn't work. It makes things worse.

After five slugs, Don makes his way upstairs. He lies down on top of his covers with his left foot planted on the floor to keep the room from flying around. That doesn't work, and soon he is sick. He bends over the toilet, hoping his demons have been exorcised.

He washes up and returns to bed and closes his eyes. The room steadies. Finally, Don starts to drift off.

And then the dreams come. It is really just one dream that turns into a nightmare and repeats itself, each time getting darker and more searing, such that after he wakes he cannot shake it. It follows him around like a heavy black cloud that precedes a bolt of lightning and the crack and roll of thunder:

Don is late for a regular session with John at the office at church. His mind is wandering in the car and he misses a turn and gets lost on streets that look strange, even though he is sure he is still in Asheville. The people on the sidewalk stare at him as if he is an alien. When he presses the gas pedal, his car does not accelerate. The steering fluid must be low and he has to turn the wheel hard to make corners. He pulls in the church parking lot but there is not a space avail-able, until a black hearse creaks slowly out. Don walks briskly to the usual room, knocks, and opens the door, saying I'm sorry I'm… Oh, I'm sorry… as he sees it's not John but Dr. Porter in the room. He's down the hall, Porter says. Don shakes his head and zigzags down the hallway where all the doors are closed. At the end of the hallway, he sees a picture of Jesus hanging on the wall and, right next to it, a door with a red sign lit up over it saying NO EXIT. Finally John walks around a corner that Don does not know is there and Don again says I'm sorry I'm… but John cuts him off and says it's no problem. So they go into an empty Sunday School classroom for children with paper cutouts in primary colors and John starts talking in words that run into and over each other. Don can hardly make it out but he's pretending to follow along the words about a formless void that was covered in darkness until there was light and you have to separate the light from the darkness only you can do that because thy kingdom come thy will be done and I'm finished with you you're just wast-ing my time. Don is looking down at the carpet and when he hears these last words—or at least thinks he does, since it was all running together—he looks up and it isn't John but the banker who was Don's friend in college. He is not friendly now when he says you're way past due and I've been very patient with you especially since I was the one who got the ransom money but you have until close of business tomorrow, to which Don replies that I paid it all back, I gave you all of your twenties back, but the banker says don't lie to me Don, where's your receipt? Hey, Don says but now there is nobody in the room, which is not a Sunday School classroom but a Wednesday night supper with people stream-ing in and a woman in a red flowered dress coming right at him saying Don, is that you, it's Gloria, remember me, Gloria? Remember our night? She opens her right palm and a palmetto bug stares at Don up and down. He suddenly realizes that he does not have a shirt on and no pants only boxers and so he puts his hands over his face and walks out the nearest exit, not remembering the sign that says NO EXIT and an alarm sounds. Someone has moved his car so he wanders around the lot looking for it and hearing voices asking was that poor Don Harwood? It seems to take forever but at the same time no time at all to get home and he pulls in the driveway next to a dark house. He enters through the kitchen door and flicks the light on only to see Detective Laney sitting at the kitchen table with his back turned saying what took you so long, he's here and I'll leave the two of you to your business. Laney turns around to stand but it is not Laney at all but Billy Burns right there in Don's house with the kitchen light shining on his dirt-smeared face. Don starts to ask what he's doing there. Don't bother Billy says. I'm here to give you a little present and Don sees there's a green shoe box on the table. Billy picks it up and opens it and pulls the skull of Matthew out by the remaining strands of blond hair, dangling it like a shrunken head. You son of a .... Hold your breath and don't judge me I've already been judged by my peers and they said not guilty. You were there you heard it. Not guilty. Twice. Not guilty. Not guilty. Now we're here to judge you Mr. Harwood. I just need to ask Matthew a couple of questions. Billy holds the hair with his left hand and steadies the jaw with his right. You were such a prissy little boy weren't you, Matthew? And didn't you tell me that you got that from your father, that he's the biggest prissy sissy of them all? Billy laughs as he sticks his middle finger out of Matthew's mouth and wags it like a tongue, mocking Matthew saying my daddy is a sissy, my daddy is a sissy. Don's legs feel as heavy as concrete as he starts to charge Billy, who backs up, rears his right arm, and hurls the skull at Don. He instinctively puts his hands out to catch and then he sits straight up in bed on top of the sweat-soaked sheets with his hands clutching the balled-up cover.

———

Don has had enough. He feels a sledgehammer slam against the back of his head again and again. Even though it's not yet 7:00 a.m., he finds Laney's home number on a pad next to the phone and dials it. "Didn't you say you knew where Billy Burns lives? In Weaverville?"

Don meets Laney for breakfast in a corner booth at the Nighthawk Cafe downtown.

"I can't live like this," Don says in a whisper.

"You can speak up. Nobody's around to hear."

Just then, a fireplug of a waitress walks up and asks, "What'll y'all have, gentlemen?"

Don's hunger surprises him, and he orders coffee, eggs over medium, sausage patties, cheese grits, and white toast. Laney say he'll have the same.

Don tells Laney about the nightmares. He squeezes the back of his neck as he speaks.

"I've got to do something. This guy is just walking around free as a bird. You said 'mountain justice.' What did you mean?"

"All I meant was getting even. Could take a variety of forms. But you understand there's risks. May not go as planned. You may get hurt. You may get caught. Remember, in the eyes of the law, he's innocent."

"But in my eyes he's guilty as hell, and those are the only eyes I can see through."

Laney tells Don that he's been keeping his eye on Billy, who runs his uncle's 'shine every Thursday night, so that the customers will be stocked up for the weekend. He also knows that there's bad blood between the Burns clan in Weaverville and the Hendrix clan in Mars Hill, who are trying to cut into the territory that Billy's uncle has always controlled. There's more money at stake than you'd expect because it isn't just 'shine anymore, it's hard drugs like acid, cocaine, mescaline, you name it, a trunk full of it each week.

"So?" Don is not sure where this is going.

"So, if something were to happen to Billy, it would be reasonable for investigating law enforcement officers to think it was a hit by the competition."

"And what would happen to him?"

"What do you want to happen to him?"

"Here ya go, gentlemen," the waitress returns and slides two hot plates across the table. The steam is still rising off of the grits as she refills the coffee cups.

When she is out of earshot, Don sits back, takes a deep breath, and stares at the food and then at Laney. "I don't just want him to hurt."

In the graying evening, Don drives to the cemetery. The elms, skeletons of themselves, reach for a sky that is falling in tiny flakes. The street lamps bordering the drive cast pools of light on the new, downy snow. Don's shoes crunch towards the grave of his son. A white blanket indiscriminately covers the graves. He stands by his son's. The covered mound makes it appear like someone is sleeping peacefully under the blanket. Don folds his hands in front of him. The flakes stick to his shoulders and forearms. He looks up, searching, and begins to say something, or ask something, not yet formulated into words, but when he parts his lips the flakes chill his tongue, and he looks down again at the silent, smooth, white mound. He kneels beside it.

"Matthew, I don't know what to do. I want you to be proud of me. It seems like all my life I have just let things slide by. I guess it's how I manage. I don't react to things. Some things, important things, I don't even feel. Your mother does. She's on the other end of the spectrum, feeling everything. Maybe that's how she and I got along, balancing each other out. Until this.

"If you can hear me, tell me what you want me to do."

But Matthew, sleeping under the white blanket that covers all, doesn't tell. The snow falls flake by silent flake.

Don rolls off his knees onto his back. He rests his head on the lower contour of the little mound and stretches his arms and legs out. He closes his eyes. He listens.

"You should be a man you could call a man."

Don bolts up onto his knees then his feet. There is no other sound. He looks but there is no one around.

"A man you could call a man? What is that?"

Don listens again and waits and looks. Hearing nothing, seeing nothing, for there is nothing more to hear or see, Don says, "I love you, son.

I always have and I always will." Then he starts to retrace his footprints, slowly, crunch by crunch.

He looks back and sees that he has left a snow angel, like the ones he and Carrie taught Matthew to make before they all got chilled and went inside to build a fire.

He leaves Matthew with his angel and heads home.

The next day Don opens the mailbox and finds among the usual utility bills an envelope addressed to him but with no return address. The handwriting is a neat cursive. Inside, he finds a one-page letter. He sits at the kitchen table and reads:

> Dear Mr. Harwood:
>
> I am the Public Defender who represented Lawrence Johnson in the criminal case and helped him obtain immunity from prosecution if he would testify against Billy Burns. I feel like I served him well, as I was supposed to do as his lawyer. The reason that I am writing to you is that I feel horrible about the result of both of them getting off. Mr. Johnson apparently has left town to parts unknown. Mr. Burns can never be prosecuted again for this crime, so he is free of it forever. The system should be that at least one of them is punished for the unspeakable thing they did to your son. I am a part of that system, and it simply didn't work. This whole episode has made me ashamed of my profession. I wish there was some way to bring justice to you. All I can say now is that I'm so sorry for your family. I hope you can find peace somehow, someday.
>
> Sincerely,
>
> Susan Troxler

Don refolds the letter and puts it back into the envelope. He opens the refrigerator, grabs the neck of a Budweiser, twists the top off, and guzzles half of it. Maybe she'll represent me, he thinks.

It takes two more meetings at the Cafe before Don and Laney finish their plan. They go over each step, repeating who is supposed to do what when until it is ingrained in them. They are ready, and their resolve is unbroken. Don keeps seeing Billy laughing at him and dangling Matthew's skull. Laney is at peace with the belief that, at the end of his long career, he will be a more direct and efficient instrument of justice than the delay and error of the law. And besides, Billy Burns is just a bunch of atoms waiting to be scattered in the wind.

Before they end their last meeting, Laney says he's thinking about a slice of the blackberry pie and asks Don if he's up for one.

Don picks up the menu and puts it back in the slot behind the napkin holder. He leans back. "You know, I can't think about blackberries without thinking of picking them when I was a kid with my grandma where she lived outside of Statesville. And I can't think of picking them without thinking of the July heat and chiggers and ticks and snakes under the bushes. That's kinda the way it is, isn't it, good with bad and bad with good? Anyway, makes me anxious whenever somebody asks me if I want blackberry pie, so no thanks."

By 9:30 on Thursday night, the cold, heavy rain starts to lighten to a drizzle. It's not quite freezing but feels like it when the wind whips up.

Billy Burns sits backwards in a kitchen chair while his uncle's girlfriend tries to fix up the black mole on the nape of Billy's neck. He's been scratching it bloody, and she pours cold rubbing alcohol on it, which makes him jump up and shout, "God dammit to hell, Louise!"

"Sorry, this ain't no fun for me either, just trying to help."

After he takes a long drag of some new stuff and pops the top of a 16-ounce Budweiser, Billy steers his Impala Coupe out of the driveway onto the slick asphalt road that leads south out of Weaverville. The cargo in the trunk is stashed under a fake bottom, cushioned by wadded-up newspapers. Billy can run his route in less than two hours and has done it so many times that he could do it more or less asleep. Tonight he turns on the radio and hums and sings along: *purple haze, all in my brain, lately things they don't seem the same, actin' funny, but I don't know why, excuse me while I kiss the sky* . . . . He relaxes with his right arm stretched out on top of the bench seat. He steers with his left hand holding the knob he screwed on to the wheel.

Billy stiffens and sits up, with both hands on the wheel, when he sees the red police light flashing in his rear view mirror. The raindrops on the rear window multiply the red lights.

"*Sheeee. . .it!*" He clicks the radio off and begins to slow down and pull to the shoulder. "I wasn't speeding, so what the fuck?!"

As a gesture of innocence, he takes the initiative to open his door and step out before the cop gets out of his car. He leaves his motor running. It is still drizzling as he looks back into the red light and the high-beam headlights. Outside of those lights, everything is black and blurry. The cop gets out and starts to move toward him. He is not in uniform. The cop stops about 15 feet away from Billy and barks, "Hands up. Face the car. Legs apart." The voice is faintly familiar. Billy begins to comply but vaguely makes out that there's another man in the police car. The fear flashes through his mind that it may be the Hendrix twins with a stolen red light. When he's been pulled over for speeding before, this is not how it has gone down. They just ask for license and registration and write you up and you get to pay a fine and they add some points on your record that would jack up your insurance if you had any. This is definitely not right.

The cop takes a couple of steps toward Billy, who is facing his driver's door, and says firmly, authoritatively, "All right, now slowly, put your hands behind your back."

Billy starts to slowly lower his raised arms. But he panics at the click of the handcuffs, especially if these guys are Hendrixes. His left hand grabs the handle, and he jerks the door open, jumps in, and shifts from park to drive while flooring it. He fish-tails out with his rear tires spewing gravel like shrapnel that spray hard into Laney.

"*Bastard!*" Detective Laney yells. He draws his revolver but Billy is quickly out of range. So he hustles back to the Ford Fairlane, tells Don to hold on, and begins the chase.

Billy is not at ease with his head start. He hits 80 in a short straight stretch on the two-lane paved road before cutting the corners of the uphill curves. He keeps one eye looking ahead and the other looking in the rear view mirror. Nothing yet behind him but he is totally spooked and presses down on the gas. Over the gap, he slows down on the downhill curves, still cutting every corner. He's looking ahead and back at the same time and accelerating past 65.

He doesn't see the shallow pool of rainwater in a dip. His front tires ski and the car hydroplanes. Billy turns into the direction of the slide but has no traction. His right front digs into the soft shoulder and the Impala Coupe flips side to side and slams into a hickory tree.

Billy is hurled across the seat and feels a wicked pain as his right leg cracks into the right door. The wind is knocked out of him and he can't take a breath. In less than a minute, the dreadful smell of gasoline sets off alarm bells in his head and propels him to breathe and get out. He reaches into the glove compartment for his pistol and is climbing out of the driver's side window, now facing straight up, when he sees the red light coming fast.

First Laney sees the steam rising from Billy's car off the side of the road. Then he sees Billy trying to climb out of the side window, which is now on the top of the car.

"There he is, the little bastard!" Laney tells Don as they slow down and pull over with bright lights shining on the wreck and on Billy. "Looks like he's hurt."

Don has nothing to say. He feels his stomach rising into his throat.

"Wait here for now." Laney instructs. He gets out and points his flashlight at Billy, who falls to the ground and, grimacing in pain, stands up holding the back of his right leg.

"Don't shoot," Billy begs. "Don't shoot."

Laney keeps Billy in the spotlight and advances to within 20 feet. "You're not getting away this time." Laney keeps advancing and reaches to the back of his belt for the cuffs.

Billy pulls his hand off of the back of his leg and points his gun at Laney's chest. He pulls the trigger three times and is dead-on with each shot: two to the chest and one to the head.

Just like that, *bam-bam-bam*, Laney is gone, forever gone, even before he crumbles to the pavement.

Through the rain-speckled windshield, Don sees everything: the hell-fire from Billy's gun, Laney crumpling in front of the Fairlane hood. He has never seen anyone get shot before, and he is horrified beyond belief to have seen the back of Laney's head explode. It does not take experience to know that that shot is instantly fatal. Just a few moments earlier, Laney was sitting an arm's length away protecting Don and telling him to wait here. Don sits, alone, mouth agape, unable to speak.

The acrid gun smoke clears and Billy sees the only witness to the shooting staring at him through the blurry windshield. Billy can't make him out. His first instinct is that he'll have to take him out, too, but then he decides that that other cop must be armed and trained and calling for back-up. So he quickly decides to run and hide, except that he can't run so well with his leg. He half-drags it as he disappears briefly into a cut tobacco field and then tries to head up the wooded hill he just came down. He slugs along because of his leg and the slippery leaves and pine straw. He stumbles and falls and gets covered in black mud.

Don is still stunned and frozen in the seat. This was not their plan, nothing close. But he can't just sit there forever. He could try to use Laney's radio, which Laney turned off, but he doesn't know how. He could pull Laney's body into the car and drive to the station. He could just walk away into the dark to the nearest house and call 9-1-1. He could just walk away into the dark and figure out a way to make it home somehow and go about his business. When police eventually show up, they'll conclude that Laney was on some undercover assignment and was trying to nail a bootlegger, who shot him, left the booze and drugs in the trunk, and fled. That was the most prudent plan, just leave the scene and to move on discreetly to an unfulfilled, lifeless life.

The back of his head pounds severely, and the throbbing pain makes him think his head will explode. He sees Billy with the dangling skull, taunting him with little prissy sissy, prissy sissy. He hears Carrie's voice telling him to *do* something, damn it Don, just *do* something!

"It can't end this way," Don resolves. "It can't end this way."

Don gets out and goes over to his friend's body. There is not much blood because Laney went out so quickly and completely. With his fingertips, he closes Laney's eyes. Laney is twisted slightly sideways, such that Don can remove his revolver without disturbing him. The body is already off the pavement, so he doesn't have to drag it.

Armed with the revolver, an eight-inch hunting knife that Don took just in case, and a surging, boiling-blood anger at the scum of a man who killed his son and now his friend, Don heads out to where Billy disappeared.

"If I am ever going to do something, it's here and now," Don vows to himself, to Carrie, to Matthew.

The wind scatters the clouds and an almost-full moon lights up the cut tobacco field and the woods. Don surveys the low field and sees nothing. Someone who is running won't stay in the open. So he starts into the thickness of the mountain forest. When the sky darkens, he waits. When the moon comes back out, he moves forward, trying not to crack branches or otherwise broadcast where he is.

Billy finds an ancient tulip poplar tree and huddles behind its massive trunk. He has three shots left, and he listens for any sound that might be a pursuer. If there is one, he will have to spot them first and then wait until they are close enough to make the shots count. He thinks 50 feet, at most. His leg, meanwhile, is killing him. He can feel it swell and stiffen.

Don moves slowly up the hill when the moon emerges. He looks straight ahead for any sign of movement and does not see the branch on the ground, which cracks with a loud report when he steps on it. "Damn!" He says inside of himself. He listens but hears nothing except the whoosh of the wind high in the white pines.

Billy sits up when he hears the crack. He waits until he hears feet shuffling before he peers out from behind the trunk. He sees a shape moving in his direction. Billy counts to ten, steps out, and fires twice.

The first bullet hits the side of a tree close to Don and scatters bark on him so hard he thinks he's been shot. The second bullet rips through the outer part of Don's left shoulder but misses the bone. "*Damn!*" Don shouts as he tumbles to the ground and seeks cover. He crawls behind a fallen oak. His shoulder is burning and bleeding, but the adrenaline keeps him focused on Billy. He switches the safety off and waits.

The intermittent moon reappears. Don notices a couple of baseball-size rocks within reach of his right hand. He quietly positions himself and hurls them, one after the other, to the left. He sees Billy step out from behind the tulip poplar pointing his gun, searching for a shape. Don steadies the barrel of Laney's revolver on the fallen oak, holds his breath, finds Billy in the sights, and pulls the trigger. He sees Billy grab his gut, hears him let out a guttural scream of "*Ahhhhshiiit,*" and watches him crumple back behind the trunk.

Then all is quiet, except for brief flutterings of the wind.

Don's heart races and he presses against his shoulder to try to stop the bleeding. He gets light-headed like he's going to faint. And, within a few minutes, he passes out in the darkness as the clouds move back in front of the moon.

———

At dawn, from high in a nearby white pine, a great horned owl calls out. The call wakes Don from a dream in which he was floating among the clouds but readying himself to land. He opens one eye and sees the blood all over his hands and shirt. He quickly remembers where he is and that sets his heart racing again. He tells himself to be calm. He starts to roll over slowly but finds that his left arm is numb and won't move. He pats his left shoulder and looks to see how wet his right hand gets. There is not much fresh blood. At least the wound is not leaking too badly, with his shirt stuck to it. Without making a sound, he looks to the trunk of the tree where he last saw Billy. It's getting lighter by the minute, and Don can see that Billy is still there. His shoes stick out the right side of the trunk and his head and shoulders stick out of the left side. He's lying on his stomach. It appears that his arms are underneath him. Don listens and thinks he hears a groan, a low groan like a call from the seventh circle of hell.

Don alternates between a light, swimming head and a keen focus. He has no plan for this. In the plan, Laney was always with him as a guide and protector. He hears another hellish groan.

Don leans back against the fallen oak and looks up. The sun, still behind the mountain, shines on the soft, white-pink cumulus clouds as they sail by looking so clean and fresh. They always change but stay the same. They are the same clouds he saw as a boy, the same ones Matthew saw.

And here am I, Don thinks. He looks up. What am I supposed to do now? The man who killed my boy is shot and lying just over there. He killed my friend last night. The man is nothing but a bunch of atoms randomly stuck together until they fly off somewhere else. But John says he's a child of God, just like me. He has dark spots, just like me. John says the Book of Matthew says if I don't forgive him, God will not forgive me, and I will never find the peace that my Matthew would want me to have. If I kill him, will I be no better than him, both of us murderers. Am I a man or a wolf? I followed the rules, and look where it got me. How can I forgive the man who robbed Matthew of his life? Even if I wouldn't forgive him for his sake, but for mine. He doesn't deserve it, but I do. In the name of Matthew, what should I do?

As Don sits there in the dawning light, his resolution softens with the pastel colors. Who am I to judge? I can just walk away and turn him in and surely he'll get the electric chair for killing a police officer.

The clouds sail by and lighten and darken the wooded hillside.

Then he sees the skull dangling from the remaining strands of radiant, golden hair. He hears Billy's taunt. Then he hears Matthew calling in the forest: "Daddy?" Then Carrie slapping the kitchen table and barking: "Damn it, Don, *do* something!"

So this is it.

He crawls quietly and slowly on the mushy forest floor, using his right elbow and both knees, toward Billy, whose groans die down. Don grips the revolver in his right hand and is ready to fire as Billy comes into full view. He pauses to see if there is any chance Billy will awaken and fight.

Billy remains face down and still. Don kneels by his side. "Thy will be done," he says to himself. He tosses Laney's revolver to the side. Using only his right arm and all the strength that he has left, he rolls Billy over and sees the pieces of leaves sticking to the dry blood that trickled from the side of his mouth.

Billy's eyes open as slits in his mud-smeared face. He squints through the haze to see who it is, but otherwise he remains motionless. Don doesn't know if he's playing dead.

Don moves one knee over to top of Billy and straddles him. He looks directly into Billy's pinched eyes. "I am Don Harwood. You killed my son and thought you got away with it."

Don's heart thumps like a barbarian's war drum. *Thump! Thump! Thump!*

He sits back on Billy's belly, pinning his arms with his knees. "Some people have told me that you are entitled to the grace of God and that I should forgive you."

Billy's eyes start to widen. He tries to open his mouth, but his lips are glued shut by the blood.

Don feels more sure of himself than at any time in his life. He knows what he has to do and he is resolved to do it. He removes the hunting knife from its leather sheath. *Thump! Thump!*

"But I don't think I can let that happen. Not for a worthless son of a bitch like you. There is not a spit of God's grace left for you."

Thump! Thump! Thump!

Don twists the knife above Billy, who through caked eyelashes sees it flash blindingly in the morning sunlight. He tries to squirm away but is spent and pinned down.

"You see this knife? It was my son's. I gave it to him on his last birthday, when he turned ten."

"I didn't do it," Billy tries to plead in a husky voice, finally able to part his lips in panic. "He just walked off. I didn't kill him! Please!"

Don leans down so that his face almost touches Billy's.

Billy tries to say, "I'm going to be a...," but the words are unintelligible gurgles.

Don's breath is hot as he says, "These are the last words you will ever hear. Listen very carefully. I do this *gladly* in memory of Matthew."

Don rears his right arm back and comes down with all the force he can muster, plunging the knife deep into the heart of the man who killed his only son. The knife goes in soundlessly, and Don twists it, cracking a rib bone, until he is sure. *Thump!*

Don pulls the knife out, rolls off Billy, and looks out, past a clearing. A calming peace comes over him. Whatever may come, he thinks, whatever may come, I'll not deny this. His body uncurls and relaxes. He does not feel his arm or any pain as he closes his eyes.

———

The morning remains still, until a dog barks from the field below.

Don hears a tiny, distant human voice say what he thinks is, "There. That way."

He moves to his knees and pushes himself up with his one good arm. He does not recall sheathing the knife, but he must have. He stoops next to Billy and picks up Laney's gun. As lightly as he can, he walks off in in the opposite direction from the bark and the voice.

He has no plan for this, but somehow he seems to know where to go. He should be drop-dead tired, but he finds renewed energy from some source, or maybe it finds him. He walks up the hill and then down to a creek, where he sees a small trout spy him before muscling away upstream. He bends over and washes his hands in the frigid water. Gingerly, he takes off his shirt and shivers to the bone as he tries to rub the blood out. The clear water turns crimson in a swirling eddy until he splashes it to allow the current to spirit his blood away. Surprisingly, the cold water gets the shirt half-clean, and it helps that it is plaid so that the colors blend in. He dabs water on his wound, which feels like he poured gasoline on it and lit it. He takes ten deep breaths, counting each one, and recovers. At least it's not bleeding badly now, even though his heart still races.

Then, shirtless, he sloshes step-by-step in the rocky creek, following it downstream. After a hundred steps and missteps, with his feet becoming increasingly numb and heavy, he sees a path running alongside and takes to it, one water-logged step after another. He slows but does not stop, thinking that if he stops he will not start again.

But he does stop once. He sees a hollow in an aging oak tree about 20 feet up the bank from the path. He struggles to the tree and drops the gun in the hollow, and it falls a couple of feet before it clunks out the bottom of the trunk. He stuffs leaves, bark, and rocks into the hole and smooths out the ground to look undisturbed.

Before noon, the creek takes a turn and intersects a bridge. Don is pretty sure, but can't be for certain, that the road above is a different one from last night. He splashes some creek water on his hair in an effort to tame it. He struggles to put his shirt back on but manages, and tucks the tail in with his right hand. On wobbly legs, he climbs up the embankment.

The day is clear and brisk as he puts his thumb out, accompanied by the most unassuming face he can put on. It is not long before a whiskered farmer with whiskied breath slows down his Ford F-150 and rolls down the passenger window with a "where you headed?"

"Just back to campus at UNC-A. I got turned around and missed my ride. Thanks for stopping."

In his bathroom, Don pours rubbing alcohol on his wound every two hours. He accepts the fact that he cannot see a doctor, unless it gets infected and starts to turn funny colors, because a doctor would have to report a gunshot wound, wouldn't he? He accepts that the fact that he will forever have a gouging scar. It will be his badge of honor.

At seven, noon, and six, he listens to the local news reports of a Weaverville bootlegger who apparently killed a pursuing Asheville detective and tried to escape but died nearby of a gunshot wound in the abdomen and a stab wound to the heart. The emphasis is on the tragic loss of the detective and the street value of the seized drugs. At the end of every report, however, there is a hook that the police still can't put all the pieces of the puzzle together, for example whether there was a second bootlegger who fled, and how to explain the missing service revolver and the knife. There is the sincere pledge to bring breaking news when it first comes available.

Don has to sit on his desire to attend Detective Laney's funeral. He convinces himself that he would stand out like a sore thumb and that someone might bump into his sore shoulder. So he watches the news report and sees the color guard and the flag-draped casket and the uniformed officers lined up breathing clouds into the cold air. He pours the last shot of Johnnie Walker and holds it up to the TV: "To you, my friend."

It takes four days before Don is ready. He leaves at six thirty in the morning to avoid the traffic and drives to the Fritzwater Institute. It is one of the coldest days that winter, and, even going slowly, his tires spin on patches of black ice. He parks close to the entrance and puts a bulky coat on top of his shoulders to obscure his injured arm.

Inside is quiet. It is not official visiting hours yet, and the receptionist is not at her desk. A fake and forlorn Christmas tree stands alone in the corner, lights unplugged.

Don walks to Carrie's room without encountering anyone, opens the door into the darkness, steps in, and closes the door behind him. He sees that she is sleeping.

Don pulls up a chair and sits beside her. Even in the dim light, he watches the covers gently rise and fall with her breaths. If you do not know about the ghosts inside her head, you'd think she was just fine. He places the hand of his good arm on her pillow and touches her hair. She doesn't notice.

The overcast sky lightens the room slightly from behind the curtains. Don can make out the shapes of the watercolors, and he sees a blush of rust on a robin's breast. He hears the officious clicking of heels as someone passes down the linoleum corridor outside. Then the clicks taper down, and silence hovers in the room again.

He stands and looks Carrie over in the gray light. She is positioned off-center on her bed, leaving him just enough room. He crawls in and lays down on his right side. His head rests on her night-gowned shoulder. Through a slow and purposeful effort, so as to disturb neither his wound nor Carrie, he is able to move his right hand to hold her left, and, so situated, he softly compresses the hand he took in marriage.

Carrie moves, barely, then remains still, as does Don.

After minutes pass, he sighs and speaks to her.

"Hey. I'm here. I did something. I evened things out."

Don thinks he feels a slight quiver in her hand.

"I had to do it. I couldn't live with myself if I didn't do it. I hope you understand, someday, even if I have to answer for it."

Soon enough, a nurse numbly follows her routine, walks into the still-dim room, and opens the curtains. She turns to the bed and says. "Oh, my!" Then she exits and closes the door almost to.

It's quiet again, until Don whispers, "It's just you and me now."

As the Assistant D.A. enters the conference room, the D.A. tells his secretary he is not to be disturbed unless the Governor calls. Then he closes the door.

The D.A. says, "Have a seat, Jim. You know we are looking like a bunch of idiots, like the gang that can't shoot straight. The press is asking me what we've found out, and I don't have anything to say except we're still looking and asking. So I need some answers."

"Ok. Here's what we've done," the Assistant D.A. says. "We got a warrant for the uncle's place and busted him and his live-in for every drug and alcohol law that's on the books. That's our leverage to squeeze them for info. And we've squeezed hard—you don't want to know how hard. But there's no juice. Nothing. They were all hunky-dory together. Billy Burns wasn't skimming them, and they were running a very profitable little enterprise. All got along fine. Said Billy always did the drop-offs alone. Nothing points to them setting out to get Laney.

"So then we rounded up every Hendrix in that part of the county. We arrested two of them, but same thing. They may have had it in for Burns and his uncle, but not for Laney. Doesn't make any sense for them to make more trouble for themselves, and, of course, Laney wasn't on that beat.

"So we talked to everybody who lived within two miles of the incident. Nothing. Didn't see anything. Didn't hear anything.

"We went through Laney's stuff at his home. Nothing to speak of. Led a pretty Spartan life.

"We checked all of the past convictions within the last five years where Laney was the key witness for us, and all of the perps are still locked up. So, I'm seeing a lot of dead ends."

The D.A's arms are folded tight across his chest, and his bushy eyebrows are forming a wide V. "What about the gun? Laney's gun? Ballistics said it was his gun that shot Burns. And it was nowhere to be found? Did it grow wings and fly away? And the knife? Autopsy said there was a stab wound an inch and a half wide. That's a pretty big knife, and it just flew away, too?"

"That same day, the police had the K-9 and the metal detectors sweeping the whole hillside. The dogs led to a creek but lost the scent there. They just started circling around and then sat down. So they called that off."

"Jesus! I'm supposed to tell the press everything went poof?"

"I don't see why you have to tell the press anything."

"This is why I'm the elected District Attorney and you're the Assistant D.A. I have an obligation to inform the public and keep their faith and trust in the system. It's not just about catching and convicting the bad guys. It's about respect for the proposition that we know what we're doing."

"Anything else?"

"You tell me. What have you *not* done?"

"I've racked my brain, and there's nothing else. I'm sorry. Laney was my friend as well as yours. I tried three cases with him, and he was always good and straight." The Assistant senses the meeting is over, or at least it's not getting any better for him, and he gets up. The D.A. resumes his crossed-arm, frowning pose, and does not stand.

As the door opens, the D.A. swivels his chair and asks, "Did you have them fingerprint Laney's car?"

"No. Why would we? There was no sign of Burns getting into the car."

"Do it."

———————

Saturday morning, Jack McNamara and his high school son park their pickup close to the bridge that spans a creek just west of Weaverville. The son carries an ax and their paper-bag lunches. Jack heaves the Stihl chain saw out of the back. They make enough selling firewood next to the Exxon station to make it worthwhile.

They hike in through the thickets and find the path that leads upstream. Jack saws the trunks, and his son trims off the small limbs with the ax. They take turns hauling the cut wood back to the truck. It's one o'clock before they rest next to an old oak tree with a hollow in it. Jack leans back and listens to the gurgles of the creek. It's so peaceful he starts to drift off, until his son gets up and rouses him.

"Ok," says Jack. "Better get this big boy down before I get pooped out. Stand back."

Jack cranks the engine and turns the whizzing blade horizontal to cut in about two feet up from the ground. He see-saws the blade side to side with just enough pressure on to keep it cutting without smoking.

Suddenly he sees sparks and hears a metal-to-metal screech. The saw quickly stops.

"What the... ?" He stops short of what he was going to say because he's trying to avoid the recent, awkward situation when his son repeated his father's loose words in front of his mother.

Jack pulls the blade free, yanks the rope to restart the engine, and begins to cut diagonally down, which is easy because of the hollow. After he opens up the side, he reaches his gloved hand into the hole and pats around. There. He grabs the hard object and pulls it out.

"*Come here!*" he yells to his son, who is standing right behind him looking over his shoulder.

"Do you remember the TV news story a couple of weeks ago about the shootings around here? A policeman, or a detective, I forget which, and a 'shine-runner were shot and killed, but they couldn't find one of the guns?"

"Yeah."

"Well, get one of those bags. We need to turn this in."

"Ok, you were right to do the fingerprints in the car, and they match the ones on Laney's gun. Problem is they don't match anybody in the system. So we know whoever was in the car with Laney may have used his revolver to shoot Burns and then took off and ditched the gun in the tree."

"A work of true genius," says the D.A.

"Well, it's just putting two and two together."

"I was kidding. It's not genius until you find the person who wears those fingerprints."

"Help me out here. Who would be riding with Laney and involved with this? Another officer? It just doesn't make any sense."

"I'm thinking on it."

It does not require much thinking. But for Don Harwood being such a straight arrow, the connection would have been so obvious that the D.A. feels like a fool. The Assistant can be forgiven because he wasn't involved in the kidnapping/murder trial, the one that the D.A. tries hard to suppress in his memory. His ears are still ringing and his face is still burning from the verdict of not guilty that sent Don Harwood toward Billy Burns in the middle of the courtroom. The D.A. has seen this before, when someone gets off and the family of the victim gets all heated and shouts out but it always goes away with time and nobody does anything so patently stupid as to hunt down the guy who walked.

As part of his new routine for Wednesday mornings before work, Don slides himself and the *Citizen-Times* into a booth at the Nighthawk Cafe.

The fireplug waitress, whose name is Becky, appears out of nowhere with a cup of coffee and the same question: "The same?"

Don looks up at her and smiles, "Yep. Why not?"

"You know, you should try us out for lunch sometime. Blackberry pie to die for."

"I'll pass, thanks," Don replies and unfolds the paper.

Before Becky returns with the breakfast, Don looks up and sees the D.A. walk in. He doesn't know that the D.A. has been having him followed for over a week so that this chance encounter was sure to take place.

Don focuses on the paper to avoid eye contact.

The D.A. casually strolls down the aisle as if looking for a table.

"Oh, Mr. Harwood, hello. I haven't seen you since the trial. How've you been?"

The two men exchange a flimsy handshake with Don starting to rise out of the red vinyl bench seat before the table catches his leg.

"I'm getting along about as well as can be expected, thank you." Don says as he sits back down.

"Say, mind if I join you for a second?" Before Don can respond the D.A. is sitting right across the table, looking straight at him.

Don's scalp starts to tingle, and the sensation runs down the length of his body. He needs to be cool and keep this short. "How have you been?" Don asks out of desperation for something to say.

"Ok, I guess. Still can't get over Detective Laney. You read about it?" The D.A. looks hard into Don's eyes, and Don can feel the look.

"Sure. Everybody has. It was tragic."

Becky delivers Don's plate, which steams with the same: eggs over medium, sausage patties, cheese grits, white toast.

"How 'bout you?" she asks the D.A.

"No, thanks. I'm supposed to meet someone and am a little early. I'll wait for them. Go ahead, Don."

"You sure?" Don asks as he is already lifting his knife and fork.

The D.A. says, "I had been meaning to call you after the trial but got carried away on other stuff. I wanted to say how sorry I was that it turned out the way it did. Still eats at me bad that the guy got off. Always tough when all you have to go on is the testimony of a co-conspirator. And I still can't figure how Laney ended up where he did, with him and the guy both shot and dead. Does not make any sense." The D.A.'s eyebrows assume a wide-V position.

Don feels the D.A.'s glare but focuses on finishing and excusing himself to get to work. But before he has the chance, the D.A. excuses himself first and says he has to get a table for himself and his friend.

"So, anyway, I just wanted to say I'm sorry, and good luck to you."

"Thanks. You, too" is all that Don can get out. Then he gets the check and gets out, trying not to look like he's fleeing the scene. Outside, he opens the door to his car and looks in the rear view mirror to see little beads of sweat covering his forehead. So much for keeping cool. But, all in all, didn't seem to amount to much. If the guy was coming at him, he would have known it.

Inside, the D.A. pats his pockets and says, "Did I leave my... ," while he walks over to Don's table before it is bussed. He nonchalantly picks up Don's knife and fork with a handkerchief and rolls them in it, puts it in his inside coat pocket, finishes his coffee, pays his bill, and leaves. He heads directly to the crime lab, where he instructs the director, who happens to be his bother-in-law, to report solely and confidentially to the D.A. whether the fingerprints on the two metal utensils match the ones from Laney's gun and car.

Don's car drives itself to the Fritzwater and he walks in like an automaton. Carrie's doctor is leaving her room as Don walks up and says, "Mr. Harwood. I was just about to call you."

They enter the room, and Don sees Carrie sitting in the chair by the window. She turns her head to see Don but does not express anything.

"For reasons I can't really explain, Carrie has made significant progress in the last couple of days, which led me to cut her dosage in half. She has been more responsive to my questions and has looked me in the eye and nodded. We're not out of the woods yet by any stretch of imagination, and she may progress in fits and starts, if she progresses at all, but this is moderately encouraging. I'll fill you in more later and let you two visit for a while. Not too much at once, ok?"

Don thanks the doctor and slowly walks over to stand in front of Carrie. He smiles at her. She still seems out of it.

Don takes her hand. "The doctor says you're doing much better. Do you feel better? Do you recognize me?"

"You're Don. Where have you been?" Her voice is old and dry.

"We have a lot to catch up on, sweetie." He sits on the bed and leans toward her. "Do you remember a while ago I came by here and told you I had evened things out?"

She turns her head to the watercolors on the wall and attempts to point her finger at them. "Why are *they* here?"

"I did something good that some people might think is bad. But I have to decide if I'm going to hide from it or face the truth."

"Where's Matthew?"

An attendant knocks on the door while pushing it open and announces that its bath time.

Don stands, leans over Carrie, and kisses her lightly on the cheek. "I'll come back later. Keep getting better. I love you. Only you."

No longer in a daze, Don swings by Quality Furniture to show his face. Wally reports that all is well. What would he have done without Wally? Don asks his secretary how she and her family are. Then he goes into his office and shuffles some papers without reading them. He stares at the trout, forever bent as if about to spring and surge. He looks at the photo of his father and, for once, does not feel small. After an hour, he figures that he might as well go home, so he does.

On the way home, Don stops for gas. He had read about an approaching cold front, and while he is pumping gas, the wind starts to whip up and blows grit and scraps of paper in small whirlwinds on the asphalt. The sky looks torn in half: the eastern half clear and the western half a brooding, heavy blanket being pushed and pulled to over where Don stands with the cold pump handle in his hand.

At home, he picks the bills out of the mailbox and says a faint hello to the Reids, who are on their way somewhere. He tosses the bills on the kitchen counter and takes a shower, not yet officially resolved to his purpose but taking inexorable steps in that direction. He steps into dress pants and buttons up a dress shirt and looks in the mirror to watch himself tying a tie for the first time since the trial. Then he slips into his jacket and returns to the mirror. Not as bad as he thought. But is it good enough? It's been a while since he looked himself in the eye when combing his hair or brushing his teeth or even shaving without averting his own gaze. He sucks his gut in and puffs his chest out and lifts his chin.

He goes downstairs and grabs his keys and goes to find the D.A., not knowing when or if he'll return. He doesn't look back as he backs onto Sunset Parkway and drives out, turning left to head downtown to the big granite building.

Bzzzzz. "Mr. Don Harwood is here to see you. I don't see him on your list... ok... I'll tell him... It will be just a minute, sir. You can have a seat."

The D.A.'s door opens and out walks a man whom Don does not recognize.

"What a pleasure. Twice in one day. Come in," the D.A. says.

Something in the D.A.'s voice, or maybe it's just in Don's head, suggests this is not a collaborative enterprise, like it was when they prepared for Don's testimony. It feels chilly, and Don feels insignificant sitting across from the powerful man and his giant desk.

"What brings you by?"

"I was thinking about our meet-up this morning, and it got me to thinking. How was Laney killed, and how was Burns killed?"

"We know that much. Laney was shot by Burns with Burns' pistol. Burns was shot by Laney's pistol and died of that gunshot wound. Seems he would have died of it even without the stabbing, which we still can't figure out."

Don reconsiders. They may be thinking that Laney shot Burns, and that that was the cause of death, not the knife. How would they ever connect Don with Laney's gun? Don shifts in his chair and looks at all of the pictures and campaign posters on the wall, a living shrine to the D.A.

"Why do you ask?" The D.A.'s eyebrows and eyes are open, innocently inquiring, not insinuating.

Don thinks about saying he is just curious, but thinks better of it. So he stalls with, "Did they ever find Laney's gun? I read where it was missing."

"Yes, as a matter of fact, we did. A few days ago."

Don straightens himself up and sees himself as he was in the mirror at home: strong, true, whole, clean. What I did was right, he says to himself, and I'd do it again. I'll not deny it, come what may. He was my son, my only child. Is a father not allowed to set things straight when they are so horribly out of line? Could he look at himself in the mirror every day for the rest of his life if he had just let it go? He is resolved to let it all out, and proudly so.

But before he can, the D.A. can't help himself. "I know why you're here, and we can stop this crap. Laney's gun has your prints on it, and it was found hidden in a hollow tree, obviously put there by someone running away from a murder scene. Your prints are also in Laney's car. The way I figure it—and you don't have to say anything because I'm not asking you to—is that you were there when Burns shot Laney and you saw Burns take off and you pursued Burns up that sloppy hill and somehow managed to shoot him dead and likely stabbed him for good measure before you got scared and took off, waded up the creek, ditched the gun, and found a way home.

"Now, why in God's name you two were out there together chasing Burns I have no earthly idea. But let's just assume I'm right about all of this, or at least 80% of it. There's such a thing as the civilized rule of law that doesn't let you or anybody else take out their personal revenge, no matter what spurred that revenge. That's what the courts are for, and juries, and judges, people without a built-in grudge to determine right from wrong. The rule of law says that Burns was innocent. But I know he was guilty. You know he was guilty. But the damn jury found him not guilty. And that's the definition of guilt or innocence—what the jury decides. If I'm figuring this mostly correctly, you shot and killed someone that the jury determined was an innocent man, and I have to decide whether to get you indicted. And I don't want you to say anything because I haven't read you your rights. Don't say anything."

As the D.A. speaks, Don sees right through him, through the wall, to the clearing sky and the pink underlines of the soft cumulus clouds. Somewhere beyond those clouds are the blue Smokies. Strangely, he feels better than he has in the two long, horrid years he has endured: he feels brave, justified.

"I don't need you to read me anything, and I don't need a lawyer. I did it, more or less like you just said. I feel so badly about Laney. He was my friend. He went out of his way to comfort me. Him getting killed, that was never supposed to happen. And I'll suffer to my dying day knowing that he fell. I'll never rid myself of the sight of seeing him shot in the head. That was never in the cards.

"But I'll tell you this: I feel no remorse, no guilt, no conscience whatsoever in killing the man who killed my son. As you just said, you know he did it as well as I do. You told me so before the trial. Hell, you indicted him. And he walked away scot-free, laughing. I just couldn't let that stand. I tried to. I tried to let it go. Talked to preacher-types about forgiving it and being a bigger person for doing so.

"I could not let things stand as they were. How would you feel if every night you heard Billy Burns taunting you, laughing at you, and tossing your son's skull at you like it was part of a game? If you were in my shoes you couldn't bear it. No man could. And if he could, he wouldn't be a man. So much of my life I felt like a civilized walking shadow, a superficial, well-respected man about town. I presented well, to most people, like I was trained to do, and I could act the part, but I wasn't a man inside.

"So, there. There you have it. Simple as that. Wrapped in a pretty bow for you. I'll never deny it, because to deny it is to deny myself, and to deny my son. What I did, to even things out, is my memorial to Matthew. God rest his soul."

The D.A. settles back and rocks ever so slightly in his swivel chair. His hands are folded in his lap and he stares at them. Don knows those hands could pick up a pen and sign a piece of paper to start the process rolling in a case that would be called *State of North Carolina versus Donald Harwood,* a case for which there would be sensational publicity and a guilty plea and, just maybe, another rung in the ladder on the way to being elected Mayor of Asheville.

Slowly, though, the D.A. gets the feeling that what is bad for Don Harwood will be bad for him and what is good for Don Harwood will be good for him. He is looking at a confessed murderer, and it is his job as the D.A. to administer justice. But what is justice? Are things even enough as they are? Should his iniquities be pardoned, like the Bible says? And what will be the fallout if he proceeds? What will the good citizens and voters of Buncombe County say about this, when they read the headline in the paper: "Prosecutor Goes After Businessman Who Says He Killed Son's Murderer"? The people now think that Laney shot and killed Burns. Maybe that's a fitting end.

So he stands and tells Don, "I'm not sure if I would have had the guts to do what you did. You did justice, in a way that the law did not. I have to do justice, too. It's not just me. It's the office. It's bigger than me, and it is charged by the people of the State of North Carolina to prosecute crimes. Even so, *I* am the one who has to decide if this office proceeds, or if this conversation will be the end of the story."

Don stands and the words "I understand" come out of his mouth.

The D.A. walks the few steps around the desk and over to him and extends his hand. Don takes it, and they don't so much shake as grip tightly and look at each other, man to man.

Then Don turns for the door.

He doesn't want to go back home. He doesn't want to go back to the Fritzwater. He drives aimlessly for half an hour, fingers thumping the steering wheel. Without planning it, he ends up at Quality Furniture. Dusk is getting ready to settle down, and the workers are drifting away to their separate lives. He avoids his office and climbs onto the loading dock, where he sits alone on the concrete floor next to a discarded *Citizen-Times* and leans back against the rough brick wall to scratch his back. He pulls his knees up and wraps his arms around them. The wound in his shoulder flashes hot and causes a momentary spasm in his face, which he shakes off.

He sits as a man you could call a man, someone who does not just accept what life delivers, but who steps out of his seat in the timid crowd of observers and enters the arena scarred but unafraid to confront, come what may, no longer a doubting mixed breed but a full-blooded man, full of himself.

He picks up the paper, which has yellowed in the day-long sun. It is open to the local section, and his eye catches a photo of a woman, who holds in her lap a framed portrait of her and Billy Burns. Don hardly recognizes Billy in a tie. He reads the caption: "Planned to Wed in January."

Don then reads the line about Anna being pregnant with the victim's child.

He lays the paper down in his lap, and the proud blood that had been coursing through his veins turns cold. His shoulders slump, and he hangs his head.

"My God, what have I done?"

Despite all of his bullish talk to the D.A., just a few hours earlier, he senses a darkening wave of remorse overcome him.

"I took someone else's life. What have I become?"

He sits empty, in silence, until he asks, "And now what?"

Those questions hang in the air until they are blown off the dock and carried one after another under a company tractor-trailer with the picture of a two-dimensional Don Harwood smiling back at the real Don Harwood, who takes a deep breath of fresh resolve and lets it out as honestly as he can.

The truck sign is faded but still reads: "Don Delivers!" He wonders about that.

He lifts his eyes to the hills.

The shadow of a cloud scurries up the hillside. Then it is gone, over the top and sliding down the backside. Soon others will chase it, up and gone as well, leaving the hemlock and mountain laurel in their wake.

ACKNOWLEDGEMENTS

I am grateful for the editing, encouragement, and constructive advice of William Boggess, Sue Williams, and, as always, my wife Jamie Brownlee.